MW01713807

What Women Want

Mari Carr

Copyright 2016 by Mari Carr

All Rights Reserved.

No part of this book, with the exception of brief quotations for book reviews or critical articles, may be reproduced or transmitted in any form or by any means, electronic or mechanical, including photocopying, recording, or by any information storage and retrieval system without express written permission from the author.

This is a work of fiction. Names, characters, places, and incidents are the product of the author's imagination or are used fictitiously, and any resemblance to actual persons, living or dead, business establishments, events, or locales is entirely coincidental.

ISBN: 978-1540414045

Editor: Kelli Collins

Cover artist: Mari Carr

Print formatting: Mari Carr

Sugar and Spice

What Women Want, book 1

Ginny's thirtieth birthday is shaping up to be the worst ever, until her best friend, Ryan, takes her to the Way Down Under, a new sex club she's been dying to visit. Too bad Ryan refuses to let her see anything but the club's tasteful bar.

Sneaking off to explore, Ginny is busted by Ryan in the Voyeur Room. But instead of taking her home, Ryan intends to teach her a lesson—and immediately commands her to strip. Stunned, Ginny obeys, and embarks on a night unlike any other. From shattering orgasms in front of strangers to light bondage, Ginny endures hours of sexual ecstasy, made to succumb again and again to her wildest urges—all by her best friend.

After hiding from Ryan the rest of the weekend—resulting in delicious punishment in his office on Monday—Ginny discovers emotions in their lifelong friendship that may have been there all along. She doesn't know if she can convince Ryan of the same…but a bit of "sweet" bondage might help.

Chapter One

"Hey there, baby. What do you have sweet in those drawers for me today?"

Ginny Brooks narrowed her eyes. "I told you yesterday to stay out of my candy stash. You ate the last of the Tootsie Rolls and I really need a Tootsie Roll today."

"Yikes. That time of the month, Brooks?" Travers joked as he pulled open the top drawer of her desk.

"Bite me." She slapped his hand away before he could grab the last of the SweeTARTS.

"What's got your panties in a bunch?" Travers asked as Charlie Anderson came out of his office.

As office manager for her rag-tag bunch of engineers and best friends, Ginny and her desk were situated in the main entryway and surrounded by the three partners' offices. She was used to having no privacy.

She was also accustomed to the way none of them used first names with each other—only last names. Travers had insisted that the others start calling him by his last name in sixth grade since there was another Ryan in their class, and he refused to be referred to as Ryan T. Ginny couldn't for the life of her figure out why that request had boomeranged back on the rest of them as well. Nonetheless, she'd been Brooks for nearly two decades. Hell, even her parents called her Brooks.

She spent her days working at Travers, Taylor and Anderson Engineering, or as Ginny liked to tease them, the T and A firm. At the moment, she was wondering why she'd ever thought it would be a good idea to work with friends.

"She just got the brush-off call from her boyfriend," Anderson answered before she could say a word in response to Travers' obnoxious comment.

"The lawyer?" Travers asked and Anderson nodded. "Fucking bastard. I'm glad he dumped you. You don't wanna date lawyers. They're slimeballs."

"Just once, do you guys think you could mind your own business?"

Anderson chuckled. "Where's the fun in that?"

She leaned her head back against her office chair and sighed heavily. "I really need some chocolate."

"Shit, Brooks. Don't you have any in your secret stash? That's why I came out here." Anderson frowned.

"Don't blame me," she replied. "Travers polished off nearly half a bag of Tootsie Rolls yesterday."

Anderson turned his narrowed gaze to his partner and she smirked at Travers.

"Snitch," Travers snarled at her. "It's your damn fault for keeping that candy in the office. It just tempts me. You know I've got a sweet tooth."

Ginny rolled her eyes. "Oh that's right. It's my fault you're a pig. I should have realized. I apologize. From now on, I'll keep the candy hidden in my car."

"Don't you dare!" Anderson barked.

"Don't you dare what?" Alex Taylor asked, coming out of his office no doubt to investigate the commotion.

Ginny rolled her eyes in frustration. How these men ever got any work done was beyond her. They were nosier than a pack of old women.

"Brooks is threatening to cut off the sweets' supply."

"Don't you dare!" Taylor yelled, adding his two cents' worth on the subject.

Ginny ignored him and decided she'd better nip the boyfriend misinformation in the bud. "And for your information, I didn't get dumped. Liam was assigned a big case and he has to work through the weekend. That's all."

"Weren't you supposed to go out of town together this weekend?" Travers asked. "I thought you and the asshole lawyer were doing a romantic getaway for your birthday."

"Well..." Ginny attempted to swallow down the lump of disappointment that had been lingering since Liam's call half an hour earlier. "We'll just have to reschedule, I suppose."

Travers slammed his hand down on her cluttered desk. "Dammit, Brooks, we wanted to throw you a big party, but you said you wanted to go away for this stupid weekend with Mr. Shit-for-Brains."

"You know, Travers. He has a name. It's Liam. Would you mind trying to refer to him as such?" Ginny was used to Travers insulting all her boyfriends and usually it didn't bother her. In fact, most of the time she thought it was sort of funny. However, today she wasn't in the mood.

"Well, this is just great," Anderson added, his voice laced with annoyance. "There's no way Taylor and I would have made plans for this weekend if we'd known your boyfriend was going to be such a jerk."

Ginny grinned. "That's sweet, Anderson, but don't worry about me. Believe me, turning thirty is nothing to celebrate."

"You gotta be kidding me!" Travers looked at her as if she'd lost her mind. "We partied our asses off for my thirtieth."

Giggling, Ginny shook her head. "Travers, I'm still hungover from your birthday party and that was six months ago."

"Ah crap, Brooks," Taylor said, interrupting her laughter. "We have to leave now or we're going to miss our flight. You sure you don't want us to cancel?"

"What?" Ginny teased. "And stand up the poor McDermont twins? No way, fellas. I'm not having that on my head. You two have been bragging about this debauched double date for weeks. Besides, I'm looking forward to hearing all the disgustingly dirty details on Monday. Go. Have fun and don't behave yourselves. I'll be fine."

"'Course you will," Travers chimed in. "I'm taking you out tonight."

"Travers, you don't have to—" she started.

"To the Way Down Under Club."

"I mean, I'd really rather— What did you say?" Ginny looked up quickly, her heart suddenly racing with excitement. She'd been begging her friends to take her to the Way Down Under Club for months. It was a new, super-exclusive sex club, and Ginny had been dying to see inside the place since its grand opening. Travers, Taylor and Anderson were all gold-card members—whatever that meant—but they'd been uncharacteristically closemouthed about the place. Every time she'd tried to invite herself along on one of their visits to the club, she'd been shot down cold.

They'd teased her, saying she was too pure or too innocent for the place.

Glancing around, Ginny could see Anderson and Taylor were shocked by Travers' invitation as well.

"I accept!" she practically shouted before they could talk Travers into changing his mind.

"Good. I'll pick you up at nine." Travers gave her a heart-stopping grin that would have caused her to expire on the spot if years of friendship hadn't left her immune to it.

Still afraid Travers would change his mind, Ginny hopped up from her desk and rushed over to Anderson and Taylor. "Have fun storming the castle, guys. I'll see you on Monday," she said as she hugged them both goodbye. "See you later, Travers."

"Later, Brooks."

Travers waved as Ginny practically sprinted for the door, still afraid her jokester friend would add a quick "just kidding" to the invite and leave her all alone on her birthday. As she heard the office door close behind her without a peep passing from Travers' lips, she breathed a sigh of relief. Maybe she didn't need chocolate after all.

* * *

As Ginny drove home, she was so excited she found it difficult to concentrate on the road. She couldn't wait until tonight. It bugged her that her friends had always refused to take her to the Way Down

Under Club. She'd grown accustomed to being a solid member of their group and their uncharacteristic adamance where the club was concerned had annoyed the hell out of her. Throughout their lives, they'd done everything together. Shared everything together. Everything.

She grinned to herself as she remembered her first kiss. Charlie Anderson, in typical fashion, had been fired up about what he'd deemed an emergency. All the sixth grade boys in their class had had their first kiss, and Anderson was worried about their gang of four being left behind…

"So then Tommy Elliot said he kissed her." Twelve-year-old Charlie Anderson picked up a rock and threw it into the creek where he and his best friends were hanging out on a cool Saturday in May.

"Eww, gross! I wouldn't kiss Charlotte Parkes," Alex Taylor said.

"Well, Tommy isn't the only boy who's kissed a girl in our class," Ryan Travers added. "Joel Madison has too."

"You know, I don't plan to be the only guy in sixth grade who hasn't kissed a girl. Hey, Brooks," Anderson perked up as he looked at her, "you're a girl."

"So what?" Ginny asked belligerently. She took a step closer to Anderson, more than happy to use the fact that she was three inches taller than him to her benefit.

Anderson backed down at her intimidating move, but Travers took up the dare with a grin. "So we could all kiss you."

"You touch me and I'll punch you in the gut," Ginny threatened.

Travers laughed. "No you won't. Come on, Brooks. Be a pal. I'll give you my Spider-Man Nerf ball."

Ginny's eyes lit up at the offer. She loved Spider-Man more than anything. "You swear you'll give it to me?"

"I swear," Travers vowed.

"Well, okay. But just once each. This is gonna be so gross!"

Anderson jumped forward, obviously excited by the prospect. He bent toward Ginny, who didn't move a muscle. The second their lips touched, they both jumped back and wiped their mouths with the backs of their hands.

Taylor shook his head. "This is stupid. I'm going to the park to play baseball. See you all there." Taylor picked up his mitt and walked away.

"I'm going with him." Ginny bent down to pick up her own ball glove, but Travers stopped her.

"I didn't get to kiss you yet. No kiss, no Spider-Man ball."

"Oh yeah. Okay, well, hurry up."

Now that Anderson had achieved his goal, he seemed ready to move on to the baseball game as well. “Yeah, go on Travers. It’s not as gross as I thought it’d be.”

“Speak for yourself,” Ginny retorted, glaring at the tow-headed boy.

Travers reached over, but rather than lean in, he pulled Ginny to him by her shoulders before moving his hands to the side of her face. “Now hold still,” he directed.

Ginny seemed too shocked to do much else as Travers rubbed his lips softly against hers. The kiss, in comparison to Anderson’s lightning-fast attempt, seemed to last for hours, and when they finally parted, Ginny could only stare at Travers, dazed.

“Holy cow,” Anderson murmured. “How’d you know to do that?”

Travers grinned, grabbed up his bat and ball and took off in the direction Taylor had just gone. “I taught Charlotte Parkes how to kiss,” he shouted over his shoulder.

Ginny laughed aloud as she remembered Travers’ cocky reply. Ryan Travers was a born ladies’ man, and she felt a small measure of pride over the fact that she seemed to be the one woman on the planet who wasn’t susceptible to his charms. Probably because she knew him too well. He’d been her best friend for more than half her life, and she was looking forward to spending her birthday with him tonight. His sense of fun was infectious, and she felt the need to throw back a few drinks, laugh and relax. She'd been disappointed as hell by Liam's phone call this morning. They'd been dating for a couple months, and she'd planned this special weekend away hoping to take their relationship to the next level.

She sighed and muttered to herself. "So much for that." More and more, Liam seemed to be putting in longer hours at the firm, and she wondered if this relationship really was meant to move forward. They had a good time when they went out together, but she wasn't the type of woman to hop into bed with just anyone. Liam, typical of most of the men she dated, seemed to assume that if the first date went well, it should end in the bedroom. She had no problem negating that belief, and she knew it had cost her more than a few second dates in the past.

Ginny took the exit off the interstate and turned left, heading for her home. At a stoplight, she thought of how Travers always seemed to be the one person in her life who managed to pick up the pieces. He had the undeniable ability to make her feel better when she was sad or upset or scared, and once again she felt herself drifting back to another time when he'd been there for her…

It was senior prom night, and their little gang of four plus dates had headed to Travers' house. His parents were out of town.

She tapped on Travers' bedroom door. "Travers," she whispered. "Are you in there?"

Travers was shirtless when he opened the door and slipped out into the hallway. "What is it, Brooks? Don't tell me my parents came home."

"No," she replied, shaking her head. She knew she should be embarrassed for breaking up his make-out session with his date, but he was her best friend and she knew he'd have the solution to her problem. "I did it."

"Did what?"

"It, Travers, you know. The big It." God help her if she had to say the word "sex".

"With Erik Rogers? What the hell is wrong with you? The guy's a wimp…an idiot."

Ginny rolled her eyes at his continual insults toward her first real boyfriend. "Dammit, Travers, will you just shut up and listen to me?"

He took a closer look at her face. "Have you been crying? Did that dickhead hurt you? Where is he? I'll kill the pansy ass!"

Ginny gripped his arm as Travers started down the hallway. "He didn't hurt me. Well, I mean, not more than I expected. It's supposed to hurt the first time."

"Shit," Travers cursed and looked at the wall. For a second, Ginny thought he might punch it. He was surly and out of sorts all the time nowadays. Anderson thought Travers was stressed out about going off to college and disappointed she wasn't going with them.

Ginny swallowed back the lump in her throat when she thought of her mother taking pictures of her and Erik tonight before the dance. She'd been wearing a baseball cap to hide the fact her hair was gone. Cancer and chemotherapy were a bitch. When her mother had been diagnosed, Ginny stopped applying to colleges and started studying medical journals, trying to help chart the surest course for her mother to overcome the hateful disease. When the doctors' bills started arriving, the idea of paying for college became an impossibility. Ginny planned to get a job following graduation and to remain at home to help her father care for her mother.

"Why were you crying, Brooks?"

"It wasn't what I expected."

"Sex? What do you mean?"

"Well…" Ginny struggled to find the words to express what was bothering her. "It was always so exciting when Erik and I made out and I really wanted more. And I felt that way tonight too. I mean, it felt good before he, well, you know…got inside me. Then it hurt and then it was over."

A smug smile crossed Travers' face and Ginny instantly regretted talking to him.

"You didn't come, did you?" he asked.

Ginny shook her head. "I thought it was supposed to be this magical thing. Special, you know? I didn't even have time to pretend to like it. I mean—"

She didn't have a chance to finish her comment because Travers burst into laughter.

"This isn't funny!"

He attempted to pull himself together although he snorted back a few chuckles as he spoke. "No, it's not. An eighteen-year-old girl planning to fake an orgasm with her first boyfriend is not funny."

"Yeah, well, it's not like we're going to get many more chances to try to perfect it. He's headed to boot camp the day after graduation. That's just next week."

"I don't think you should try again at all. I've told you a million times, you and Erik are too different. He's not right for you. Let the bastard ship off."

Ginny frowned. "You're not being helpful."

He sighed heavily. "Yeah, I know. I'm sorry. I guess I just wish you would've waited. Erik's the wrong guy for you."

"I'm tired of waiting. You guys have been doing it for ages."

Travers laughed. "It's different for us."

"Bullshit."

"It'll get better, Brooks. Most girls don't come the first time. It's a problem with the female mind. You all think too much and forget to let go and have fun. I can just imagine everything that was running through your head while old Erik was struggling with the condom. Let's see, I bet you were worried about the way you looked naked, your prom dress getting wrinkled, getting caught, somebody hearing you, what your mom would say. Have I covered it all?"

Ginny giggled. "You left out the 'condom breaking, getting pregnant' one. That's a biggie."

Travers gripped her by the back of the neck and placed a kiss on top of her head. "Dear God, tell me the condom didn't break."

"It didn't break."

"Yeah, well, this little conversation just proves my point. Don't worry about it, Brooks. I'm sure the sex will get better. Probably not with the eunuch Erik—Oof! Hey, what'd you punch me for?"

"That was for Erik." She leaned up and kissed his cheek. "And that was for me."

* * *

"What the hell does that 'storming the castle' thing mean? She says it all the time," Ryan Travers wondered aloud as he watched Brooks leave the office.

"Sadly, I know the answer to that. It's her favorite line from The Princess Bride. She made me watch it with her one weekend," Taylor answered.

"Are you nuts?" Anderson yelled, clearly not concerned about Brooks' Princess Bride fetish. "What the hell do you think you're doing? You can't take her to that club."

"Why not?" Travers shrugged.

"Because it's a sex club, dumbass! This is Brooks we're talking about. Not one of your Tramps of the Month."

"You know, if I didn't resemble that remark so much, I'd punch you in the damn mouth." He laughed, but Anderson looked ready to pop a blood vessel in his brain. "Listen, why don't you give me a little credit here? It's her thirtieth birthday for Christ's sake and Loser Liam left her high and dry. We all know that she's been chomping at the bit to get into that club. I'll take her to the bar section, buy her a few drinks and deliver her home safe and sound. Trust me, she'll still be our sweet little Brooks in the morning."

"So you won't let her leave the bar area?" Anderson asked.

"What are you? Her fucking father? No, I won't let her leave the bar," Travers promised.

Taylor looked at them and shrugged. "It is the perfect present," he said.

"That's what I've been saying. So, you boys better get going or you'll miss your flight. Have fun screwing yourselves silly with the McDermont twins and don't worry about a thing here. I'll show Brooks the time of her life."

"That's what I'm worried about," Anderson muttered, but he let himself be ushered out the door by his two best friends.

Ryan watched his friends pull out of the parking lot before going back inside and meandering over to Brooks' desk. He opened her top drawer and helped himself to the last piece of candy. He really should buy a bag or two—or twenty—to replace all the sweets he'd stolen from her over the years, but that thought never seemed to cross his mind when he was at the grocery store.

As he opened up the package of SweeTARTS, he spotted an old photograph lying in the drawer. Pulling it out, he grinned to see a picture of him with Brooks and Anderson standing by a campfire and hamming it up for the camera while Taylor snapped the shot. He was amazed to see how little they'd all changed over the years. The photo was from a camping trip at the end of summer after their high school graduation, sort of a last hurrah before the guys went off to college and Ginny started her new job.

Ryan was a bit embarrassed by how often he thought of that night, the memories of it burned on his brain so that it truly did feel as if it had happened yesterday. He'd waited until the other fellas had fallen asleep…

"Scoot over, Brooks."

"Travers, what are you—"

"Shhhh, do you wanna wake up the other guys?" Ryan whispered as he unzipped Brooks' sleeping bag and attempted to crawl in.

"What are you doing?" she whispered.

"It's our last night together."

"No shit, Sherlock. Why do you think we're camping out?"

"Well, I thought I'd take care of your problem for you." Ryan curled up beside her and ran his hand along her rib cage, pleased when she shivered with delight at his touch.

"What problem?"

"Your orgasm problem," he answered simply as Brooks froze.

"Travers, I am not having sex with you."

"I never said anything about sex, just orgasms."

"What's the diff—"

"Shhhh. No more talking. And do me a favor, Brooks—try to concentrate on what I'm doing and nothing else. Okay?"

He was slightly surprised when Brooks fell silent. She was never one to give in easily, and it thrilled him that she trusted him enough to let him proceed without an argument. He even got the sense that she wanted him to touch her.

He reached down and tried to work the boxers she was sleeping in down over her hips. Anderson and Taylor were sacked out on the other side of the campfire.

Once he had her boxers past her knees, he whispered, "Kick them off or they'll be in the way."

Brooks complied and Ryan grinned. He wasn't sure why he felt so compelled to do this, but he'd sensed Brooks' disappointment ever since prom night, and he didn't want to leave for college without proving to her that sex really could feel terrific. God only knew what kind of clods she'd start dating without him around to weed out the unsavory ones. She sure had shitty taste in men.

Once she was bare from the waist down, Ryan dragged his fingers along her hip and around to her shapely buttocks. She was fit and trim and her ass filled his hand nicely.

"Open your legs," he whispered and again, Brooks obeyed without hesitation. Ryan sucked in a deep breath and struggled to ignore his raging hard-on. He pushed his waist away from her a bit, afraid she'd feel his erection and freak out.

He grabbed her left leg and positioned it over his right hip. He was aware of the fact he was mostly lying on the cold ground rather than in the sleeping bag, but all he really cared about was that Brooks was covered up. It wouldn't do for Anderson and Taylor to wake up and find him with his fingers buried in their best friend's pussy.

They lay side by side, facing each other, and Ryan could feel her accelerated breathing on his cheek. "Relax, Brooks."

"I'm trying," she insisted, "but this is weird."

Ryan chuckled and brought his fingers to her pussy. He slowly pushed his finger through her curls until he found her clit. She hissed in a breath as he touched the sensitive button.

"There it is," he whispered, increasing the pressure until she began squirming. "You like that?"

"Oh my God, yes," she replied breathlessly.

Ryan forged on and trailed his fingers down to her wet opening.

Shit, her soaked opening was more like it. She was dripping with juices and her cunt was on fire. Ryan stifled a groan at the thought of what it would feel like to push his cock into that hot pussy. He pushed one, then two fingers inside and Brooks' hips started moving against them, trying to force them farther in.

"Easy," he murmured, but she didn't seem to hear him. She was gyrating wildly on his thrusting fingers, and he was having a hard time holding back his own enthusiasm. She was so incredibly sexy it was all he could do not to come in his pants. When he sensed she was close, he moved his thumb back to her clit and tapped it firmly, twice.

He sensed Brooks wasn't going to come quietly, so he moved fast to cover her mouth with his other hand. He wasn't disappointed.

"Shhh, wildcat," he whispered, attempting to soothe her moans as she slowly came down from the peak. Glancing over, he saw that Anderson and Taylor were still sound asleep. Thank God. Brooks would have been mortified if they'd woken up.

Slowly he moved back, loving the sounds of her regretful whimpers as he pulled his fingers from her quivering pussy.

When his hand was free, she hugged him. He wrapped his arms around her and for several moments, neither of them said a word.

"Travers," she whispered, leaning back to look into his face.

"Yeah, Brooks?"

"Thanks."

He kissed the end of her nose and reverted back to his usual teasing. "Well, we men have a duty to uphold the reputation of all mankind. Couldn't let you go around thinking we were all crap in bed."

She'd given him a heart-stopping grin, and Ryan could still recall the pain he'd felt at leaving her behind.

He hadn't been ready for things to change, and he remembered the fear of losing her as a friend—terrified they would drift apart as so often happened.

He shrugged off his wayward thoughts and sighed. Luckily their friendship survived the time and distance, and tonight, by God, he was going to show her one hell of a good birthday. She deserved it and besides, that's what friends were for.

Chapter Two

The doorbell rang at nine-thirty and Brooks jumped up from the couch where she'd been fidgeting with nervousness and excitement for the past hour. She'd been a damn fool to actually expect Travers to show up on time. The man was notorious for his tardiness. They liked to joke around the office that he'd be late for his own funeral.

As she stood, she straightened her tight leather skirt and pulled down her low-cut blouse, pleased by the sexy bit of cleavage peeking out. She picked up her ID and debit card, intending to have Travers carry both in his pocket for her, and grabbed her cell phone as she walked over to open the door.

"Hey, Travers."

"What the fuck are you wearing? What did you do to your hair?"

She jerked back at the vehemence in Travers' tone, glancing uneasily at the outfit she'd only seconds before thought was perfect. "I went to the beauty salon and had them put in some blonde highlights, then I went shopping this afternoon. I wasn't really sure what the norm was for a sex club, but I thought this was okay. What's wrong? Too virginal?"

"Virginal? Shit. You look hot as hell! You can't wear that."

"Why not?"

Travers swallowed heavily as he continued to look her up and down, and Ginny wondered what was wrong with looking hot as hell. Actually, she felt a tiny grin creep to her lips at his compliment.

Having grown up with the men in her office, Ginny was used to feeling like the same awkward middle schooler she'd been when she'd met them. Never much of a girlie-girl, she'd been the tomboy they'd accepted into their midst as an equal, and it was a role that had fit her like a glove…when she'd been twelve.

Somewhere along the line her feminine side had kicked in, but by then, Anderson, Travers and Taylor had stopped looking at her as a woman, and instead saw Brooks, their buddy. The one who'd built a tree house with them, who'd creamed them in roller hockey and who'd smoked cigars with them behind the high school gym during their freshman year.

"Forget it," Travers grumbled. "Are you ready to go?" Ginny raised her eyebrows and he offered her a guilty grin before adding, "Sorry I'm late."

"No problem. I was afraid you'd changed your mind about taking me."

"What if I have changed my mind?" he asked.

"It's too late. You promised. Now let's go."

Travers shook his head and walked her to the car, crossing to the passenger side to open the door for her. She was blown away by the gentlemanly act. Usually they raced each other to the car shouting, "Shotgun!"

"I didn't," Travers said as he held the door open.

"Didn't what?"

"Promise," he replied.

"But, Travers…" She stiffened her spine, prepared to fight if necessary. There was no way he was getting out of taking her to the Way Down Under Club.

"Get in, Brooks."

She sat down as he shut the door behind her and walked in front of the car to his side.

As he climbed in, he leaned over and touched the furrowed lines on her brow with the tip of his index finger. "Don't worry. I'm taking you to the club. But I'm warning you right now—you better not get more than five feet away from me at any time. Not looking like that. I'm not sure I'll be able to beat all the men away from you."

Ginny smiled at his sweet words. "You sure do know how to make a girl feel special on her birthday. I know I haven't said it before, but thanks, Travers. I have to say this has gone from being the shittiest birthday in history to one of the best."

"Yeah, well. We haven't gotten there yet. I'm afraid you might be in for a bit of a disappointment. There really isn't much to see at the club."

"Nice try, hot shot, but you aren't going to talk me out of this."

"Why in the hell are you so fired up about going to a sex club? I thought you said the shithead didn't dump you."

"Liam," Ginny stressed his name, "and I haven't broken up. Besides, I just wanna look around the place. Nobody said anything about me going there to hook up."

"Yeah, well, believe me, dressed like that, every guy is going to want to hook up with you, whether you're looking for it or not."

* * *

Ryan tried to remember why he'd thought it would be a good idea to bring Brooks to the Way Down Under Club as they pulled up to the front door. A valet opened the door for her, and he had to thrust his hands in his pockets to keep from punching the guy in the face for eyeballing his best friend's overabundance of cleavage. Moving quickly around the car, he placed a protective arm around her back and steered her toward the front door.

"I meant what I said before, Brooks. Stay close."

She giggled and Ryan felt uneasy at the mischievous sound. "Now where's the fun in that? Relax, Travers. I'm a big girl, remember?"

Ryan fought to restrain a growl. If he had a brain in his head, he would have waited to bring her here until Anderson and Taylor could come as well. He had a feeling it was going to be tough running interference alone. Despite her insistence that she and Liam were still an item, he could see she was hurt by the fact the guy had bailed on their romantic weekend. Bringing a pissed-off Brooks to a sex club was probably not one of his more intelligent moves. He'd just been desperate to wipe away the look of sadness he'd glimpsed in her eyes this afternoon when she said Liam wouldn't be taking her out of town. He'd grasped for the first thing he could think of to make her smile and this was it.

It didn't help that she'd pulled out all the stops on her appearance either. It wasn't that he didn't think she was pretty. He'd just grown used to seeing her in loose-fitting jeans and conservative tops, and tonight her lusciously long legs in that tight skirt were making him think highly inappropriate thoughts.

On top of that, she never wore her hair down. She was the queen of ponytails and braids. Thinking back, he didn't think he'd seen her light brown hair loose since senior prom, and it had been considerably shorter back then. When did it get so thick and silky? And why did she have to add those sexy highlights? Damn if she wasn't a knockout.

He readjusted his pants and shook his head. Shit, he was getting a hard-on thinking about Brooks. What the hell was wrong with him?

He nodded to the doorman, Burt, before guiding Brooks toward the bar section of the club. There were strict rules at Way Down Under, and the main one was that there was no hanky-panky in the bar. It was a sophisticated room, decorated with black leather furniture and cherry wood. It was dimly lit and soft jazz played in the background. It was the perfect place to meet new people or have an intimate chat with a lover. The atmosphere was romantic, without the slightest hardcore sexual overtones. Compared to the rest of the place, the room was almost chaste.

No doubt, Brooks would be shocked by what she would find beyond this room. Not that she was leaving the bar…at all. They were going to have a few drinks and then he was going to take her back to her house—none the wiser about his true connection to the club.

Unbeknownst to her, her employers weren't merely members, but part owners.

"Wow," Brooks whispered as they entered the classy room. "This is gorgeous. Beats the hell out of the bar at Buffalo Wild Wings."

Ryan laughed at her joke. Her sense of humor was one of the things he enjoyed most about her. Despite the fact she'd been one of his best friends for years, he seemed to be seeing her in a different light tonight. Whether it was the romantic setting or the fact she looked so feminine and beautiful, he couldn't quite put his finger on it, but for some reason, everything he'd spent a lifetime taking for granted about her suddenly seemed illuminated, brighter, more stunning.

"Come on. Why don't we grab that table by the fireplace?" He led her to the table, painfully aware of the stares they were receiving. He seldom came into the bar, usually preferring to take his dates straight to the more interesting rooms. While he didn't think anyone would directly approach Brooks as long as she was with him, he did—much to his chagrin—see two of the club's more aggressive Doms eyeing her with some serious interest.

Terrific. He was screwed.

He pulled out a chair for her before taking his own seat. "So what would you like to drink?" he asked as the waiter immediately stepped up to take their order.

"Oh the usual, I suppose. Tequila shots 'til we drop?"

Ryan grinned and shook his head. Regardless of his unfamiliar feelings toward her, Brooks didn't seem to be sharing the awkwardness of the situation.

"Why don't we try something a bit different tonight?"

"Okay," she agreed. "I'm game. What are you thinking?"

"Have you ever had a martini?"

She shook her head.

Ryan looked up at the waiter. "We'll have two Grey Goose martinis."

"Ooh la la. Aren't we playing the part of sophisticates tonight? Should I drink with my pinkie out?"

"Very funny, Brooks. There's nothing wrong with a little high living every now and again."

"I wouldn't know. I'm a lowly office manager."

"Shit, Brooks. You run that damn business of ours and you know it. We've been trying to convince you for years to become a full partner."

"Let's don't fight that old fight, Travers. You guys have the big fancy engineering degrees—master's degrees and all that. I have an associate's degree in Business Administration from the community college and I've taken a couple of accounting classes so I can keep the books and that's it. There is no way you guys can justify making me a partner."

"Brooks, you're smarter than the three of us put together and you know it. If your mother hadn't gotten sick, you'd have gone to the university with us."

If Ryan could have bitten his own tongue off, he would have.

Great, Travers. Bring up the worst time in the woman's life on her birthday.

"Stop looking so guilty, Travers. My mother is alive and in remission and I'd much rather have her than a lousy framed piece of paper hanging on the wall. Besides, let's face it, your folks blew all that money sending you to college and it didn't make you any smarter," she teased.

"Yeah, well, it made me smart enough to hire you. We couldn't run that place without you."

Brooks frowned and looked at him so strangely he wondered what he'd said wrong.

"You know, Travers, it's kind of hard to be a smartass when you keep saying such sweet things."

Ryan shrugged. "Sorry, I'll work on being my usual charming jerk again."

"I'd appreciate it." She smiled and Ryan felt like he'd been punched in the stomach. Christ, Brooks was the most beautiful woman he'd ever seen. The revelation caught him so unaware, he felt dizzy.

The waiter returned with their drinks and Ryan was grateful for the opportunity to try to recover his wits.

"What should we toast to first?" she asked as she lifted her glass.

Ryan smiled. "First, middle and last tonight—your birthday. Happy thirtieth, Brooks."

"Thanks."

As they drank, Ryan caught sight of a couple in the corner of the room. He hadn't noticed them when they'd walked in as he'd been too preoccupied with the attention Brooks was generating.

Now, however, he could clearly see Liam the Enormous Prick wrapped around some buxom blonde.

The lawyer and his date were pushing the limits on the bar rules and were precariously close to breaking all of them in one fell swoop. Liam's hand was firmly cupped around the woman's breast and he was nibbling away at the all-too-prominent nipple poking through her tight, sheer blouse. The woman was humping Liam's thigh, and her moans were starting to make their way through the room despite the music and soft chatter surrounding them.

"What are you looking at?" Brooks asked.

"Nothing!" he answered, too loud and too late. Brooks' gaze landed on Liam before swinging back toward him. Ryan watched all the color drain from her face.

"Oh," she whispered.

Ryan could hear the pain behind the single syllable, and he fought against the urge to walk across the room and beat the hell out of her so-called boyfriend.

"Crap," she said, glancing over her shoulder once more before turning back around to face him. She picked up her martini and drained it. She cleared her throat and he could see anger in her gaze. "Do I have the word 'frigid' written across my forehead?"

Ryan shook his head slightly, certain he'd heard her question wrong. "Excuse me?"

"Frigid, Travers. F-R-I-G-I-D. Is it tattooed up there in some way that only men can see?"

"I don't understand what you're asking, Brooks."

"What is it about me that make the men I date think I'm not worth waiting for? What the hell is wrong with getting to know someone before you hop into bed with them?"

"I'm not sure," Ryan answered slowly. Her question had caught him off guard.

"I mean, even you didn't think I could handle one night in a lousy sex club. What's wrong with me? What vibes am I sending out?"

Ryan stared at her for several seconds, his mind whirling over how on earth to answer her. How could he tell her that until tonight, he'd seen her—or maybe he should say he'd failed to see her—the same way as the asshole across the room? Shit. Bringing her here had been a mistake of mammoth proportions, and things seemed to be spiraling continually downhill.

"There's nothing wrong with you."

"Oh stuff it, Travers! After nearly twenty years of friendship, the least you could do is level with me. Clearly men don't view me as sexy. Am I right?"

She thought she wasn't sexy? Christ, he'd been sporting a hard-on since she'd opened her damn front door. Even now, he was silently reciting his times tables in an attempt to stop thinking about exactly how he'd like to peel that tight leather skirt off her. Ryan picked up his drink and followed Brooks' example by tipping it up and chugging it down…fast. The strong liquor burned his throat and when he tried to speak again, his voice sounded gruff, guttural.

"Brooks, I can honestly tell you that right now, you are the sexiest fucking woman in the room."

His answer seemed to take the wind out of her sails and her anger quickly turned to something worse—sadness.

She nodded for a moment and he waited patiently as she seemed to try to pull herself together. If there was one thing he loved about her, it was the fact she didn't wallow in self-pity. She was a confident woman with none of the usual hang-ups his past lovers seemed to suffer. She knew her value and didn't need constant reassurances about her appearance, her intelligence or anything else, for that matter.

After several tense, quiet moments, she took a deep breath. "Thanks…again."

"You're welcome," he replied, relieved to see the return of her composure. God, she was a graceful woman. How had he missed this for so long?

"Well, I think I'm ready for my tour now. Let's get the hell out of here."

Her words washed over him like ice-cold water. "What tour?"

"Of the club. Surely there's a hell of a lot more to this place than just the bar."

"I'm not taking you on a tour. Shit, you're lucky I brought you this far." The words flew out of his mouth and he cursed his thoughtlessness, especially when her eyes narrowed in anger again. This time her fury was directed at him.

Somehow he preferred it when she was pissed at the idiot lawyer.

"I see," she said through clenched teeth. "So you lied to me."

Ryan refused to crumble under her anger. She'd tried to use intimidation on him since they were kids. He'd never let her get away with it then and he sure as hell wasn't starting tonight. "I told you I'd bring you to the club and I have, but I'm telling you right now, Brooks, this is all you're going to see of the place."

"How about the ladies' room? Are you going to let me see that?"

Her question caught him by surprise. "Of course you can go to the bathroom."

"Where is it?"

He couldn't understand her easy acceptance of his refusal to show her the rest of the club. "Back out the door we came in. First door on the right."

"I'll be back, Travers, and then I want you to take me home."

"Brooks—"

"And after you take me home, you can go fuck yourself."

Okay, so maybe she wasn't taking his refusal so well. Great, this is what he got for trying to be a good friend. Well, two could play the pissed-off game. "Fine, Brooks. I'll settle the tab."

Chapter Three

Ginny stormed back to the front entryway and violently shoved open the door to the ladies' room. She watched the two women inside take one look at her face before giving her a wide berth and leaving her alone in the most spacious restroom she'd ever seen. No doubt they'd seen the steam coming from her ears.

Damn Liam! The lying, two-timing scum sucker. She recalled his oh-so-apologetic voice on the phone this morning. I have to work late. Big case. I really have my hands full with this one. Oh, his hands were full all right. Full of that blonde slut's lousy boob job. She hoped he got silicone poisoning from all that disgusting slurping and mauling he was doing. Son of a bitch.

She stood in front of the mirror and tried to still the blood pulsing through her body. She had an overwhelming desire to ram her fist into something. That was one of the problems with hanging around her male friends so often. The only way she knew how to feel better was to hit something. Why couldn't she just cry and get it all out of her system like a normal woman?

The thought of her friends infuriated her even more. Fucking Travers. Regardless of his words, he had lied to her. He knew why she'd wanted to come to the club. If she'd just wanted a goddamn drink, they could've gone anywhere.

She glanced up at her image, disheartened by what she saw. She'd felt so pretty an hour ago, sexy, hot. Now she just felt old. Some birthday.

Looking in the mirror again, she saw the reflection of a second door on the opposite end of the room from where she'd entered. It opened and a woman walked in. A smile crept across Ginny's face as she glimpsed for just a moment what was obviously another entrance to the rest of the club. Hopefully, a much more interesting part.

Screw Travers. She was a grown woman and she was going to give herself the birthday of a lifetime. She pinched her cheeks, fluffed her hair, took a deep breath and decided tonight was her night. If he wasn't going to give her a tour, she'd show herself around. It would be better that way. If she met a man, Travers would no doubt find something wrong with the guy and scare him away.

Tonight she was turning over a new leaf, living a little. Hell, maybe living a lot if the room behind door number two delivered. It was a sex club, after all.

Walking over to the door, she slowly opened it and stepped into a world she'd only read about in the sexy books she kept under her bed.

The large ladies' room clearly accommodated two parts of the club, and she found herself in a dim circular room with a stage in the center. Around the darkened stage were several tables, not unlike those in the bar area. However, there was other furniture in the room as well. Chaise lounges, long couches and overstuffed armchairs were scattered amidst the more staid seating.

Ginny was grateful for the darkness as it appeared to be a full house tonight. Most of the seats were taken by couples or groups in various states of dress—or undress, as it were. Feeling rather conspicuous standing alone, she quickly scouted and found an empty table by the back wall. She claimed it, anxious to begin observing her surroundings in relative privacy.

Geez, she thought with glee. She could watch the activities of the room all night and never need whatever show was apparently going to take place on the stage. She could barely believe her eyes.

On one of the couches to her left, she watched two women wearing chains on their ankles and wrists—and nothing else—give a man dressed in black leather chaps a hell of a blowjob. Every now and then, he flicked a whip against their asses, and Ginny could hear their grateful moans as their tongues tangled together against the man's rigid erection. She wondered briefly what it must feel like to be lashed with a whip, and she felt the slightest fluttering of excitement at the thought of being chained.

At the table in front of her, a woman was sitting with her legs spread apart while a naked young man knelt between them, lapping at her pussy like a thirsty dog at a pail of water. The woman held something that looked like thin reins in her hand. Ginny squinted and realized the small chains were attached to the man's nipple piercings. The woman tugged at the chain—hard. Ginny thought she must surely be hurting the man but he certainly didn't seem to mind, if the stiffness of his cock was any indication.

She'd never thought of herself as someone who enjoyed watching others engage in sex, but her body was certainly telling her differently right now. She squeezed her thighs tightly together, trying to still the sudden ache of desire.

Holy hell, what on earth could happen on the stage that would top what was happening in the audience?

"Excuse me. Are you alone?"

Ginny jumped slightly at the sound of a man's voice. Glancing up, she saw a handsome man dressed in an elegant three-piece suit. The sophisticated clothing seemed strangely out of place in this room full of leather and flesh.

"You startled me," she said breathlessly, slightly embarrassed by the fact he'd caught her gawking.

“I’m sorry. I thought you saw me approach.” The man gave her a smug grin that let Ginny know she’d been busted. He knew perfectly well she hadn’t seen anything but the lust-fest going on around her. “I’m Marcus Steele, I manage this club.”

“Ginny Brooks,” she answered, wondering if perhaps he’d come over to toss her out. Technically, she was crashing this party. Travers was the club member and he certainly hadn’t invited her to see this room. He probably thought she’d bailed on him and had taken a taxi home. The thought of him frantically searching for her brought a smile to her face. She was still more than a bit miffed at him.

“Ms. Brooks, it’s a pleasure. May I join you?”

“Um, well, sure.” Obviously he wasn’t intending to throw her out, but at the same time, she was a little uncomfortable at the thought of sitting with a gorgeous stranger while every other person in the room was engaged in some form of down-and-dirty sex.

Of course, when she thought about it, the whole evening had taken a surreal turn. Travers’ unusual compliments, Liam’s almost comical, sloppy lovemaking in the bar and now this. She was beginning to feel like she’d stepped out of her own life and was presently starring as Alice in Hornyland.

“It’s not common to find such a beautiful woman alone here.”

"Yeah, well, about that. You see, I came here with a guy. I mean, just as friends and we sort of decided to split up, do our own thing, you know, before meeting back up again." Ginny fought not to roll her eyes at what sounded—even to her ears—like the biggest pile of shit ever shoveled.

"I see." Marcus nodded. "I must admit I'm surprised any man would leave a woman as lovely as you alone. This friend of yours, perhaps he's gay?"

Ginny burst out laughing at the thought of Ryan Travers as a homosexual. She was fairly certain a more masculine man had never walked the earth. He was a football-watching, NASCAR-crazed, beer-guzzling, pizza-ordering man's man from the word go, and she didn't even want to know how he'd react to Mr. Steele's comment.

"I'll take that as a no?" Marcus asked.

"Definitely a no. My friend is absolutely, positively not gay."

"Blind perhaps?" Marcus leaned closer and Ginny grinned at his obvious attempts at charm. Not that they wouldn't have worked on a lesser woman, but Ginny Brooks had endured millions of Travers' gorgeous, heart-stopping moves. Her immunity to such antics was almost perfect.

"Not blind either," she answered matter-of-factly. "He's just not interested."

As soon as she spoke the words aloud, she felt an unfamiliar pang of disappointment. Travers hadn't touched her in a sexual way since the night they'd gone camping after graduating from high school. She'd harbored a small crush on him for about a year after that—until he'd come home the following summer and proceeded to cut a swath through all the hometown girls before returning to college. According to Anderson, his dating record at home was only surpassed by his dating record at college. At that point, she'd resigned herself to their continued friendship, and it really didn't take her long to recover from the crush and move on.

She hadn't thought of Travers as a man she could be attracted to for over a decade. However, if she was being honest with herself, he'd gotten under her skin tonight. His sweet words, his charisma, his charm. They'd all snuck under her defenses and struck a chord.

Shit. What the hell was she thinking? There was no way she could actually desire Ryan Travers. He was her arrogant, immature, cocky friend and nothing more. That damn martini must have been more potent than she'd realized.

"Well then, he's a fool, because I can assure you it's simply not possible for him to find a more attractive woman in this club."

"Ooh, very nice," Ginny purred and she watched Marcus' eyes narrow slightly. No doubt he expected her to be easily swayed by his empty flattery.

“You’re an interesting woman, Ginny Brooks. Can I buy you a drink?” he asked.

Ginny leaned closer and reveled in the feeling of seducing such a handsome man. Clearly he was accustomed to using his good looks and charm to win women over, and she wondered if any woman had ever challenged the dominating edge she could sense beneath the surface. At last, the night seemed to be looking up.

“I’d love a drink,” she whispered huskily.

“What the fuck do you think you’re doing?”

Ginny winced as Travers barked his question from behind her. She turned slowly, sighing loudly. Looks like the bouncer had arrived after all.

“Hey, Travers,” she said lightly. “I didn’t think you’d still be here.”

“Ryan Travers?” Marcus’ voice drifted from behind her, and she glanced back in time to see a trace of humor on his face as he looked at her. “Ryan Travers is your friend?”

Ginny was confused by the question, but it didn’t matter. Travers didn’t give her time to answer.

“Yeah, I’m her friend. What the fuck is going on, Brooks? I thought you were just going to the restroom.”

“I got turned around, lost,” she lied.

“Sure you did.” His answer was accompanied by a smirk that merely reinforced the sarcasm in his tone.

"Listen, Travers, I don't need a babysitter, so I relieve you of your duties. Why don't you run along and do whatever it is you usually do in this place? I'll be fine here with Marcus."

"Marcus?" Travers' voice was laced with annoyance and anger.

"I had no idea she was with you, Ryan," Marcus said.

"He's not with me," Ginny interjected, but neither man seemed to hear her.

"Well, now you know she is," Travers answered.

"No, I'm not," Ginny insisted, but again she was ignored.

"I'm surprised you left such a lovely woman alone in the Voyeur Room," Marcus chastised.

"It was an oversight. One I don't intend to make again."

"Um, hello, I'm still sitting here. I can hear you talking about me." Ginny was becoming angry at being treated like a naughty child. "Travers, I don't know who stuck the stick up your ass tonight but as you can see, I'm perfectly fine. Marcus and I are going to—"

Marcus rose as she spoke and interrupted her comments. "It was a pleasure to meet you, Ms. Brooks. I would like to warn you, however, that should you return to visit our little club, it would be unwise to escape your host. Travers," Marcus said with a nod, "enjoy your evening."

Ginny watched with disbelief as the man quickly made his escape. Closing her eyes, she sighed heavily. She didn't bother to open them when she heard the chair beside her move and felt Travers sit down next to her.

"Brooks," he said softly.

She opened her eyes, surprised to find him leaning in so closely, only a few inches from her. She knew she failed to mask the sadness she felt as she watched the last traces of anger fade from his face.

"Some birthday, eh?" he asked with a crooked grin.

She shrugged, appreciating his attempt at humor. Somehow Travers had always been able to make her laugh, to make her problems seem less serious, her life less stressful.

"I've had better," she whispered. She glanced around, once again besieged by the strangeness of the moment. She looked back at her friend and heard the question she never thought she'd have the courage to ask fall from her lips. "Why are you a member of this club?"

Rather than pull back or shut her out as she expected, Travers leaned even closer and answered, "I was introduced to some alternative lifestyles at college. I met a woman who was into this scene. She invited me to a party and I realized I was into it too."

Ginny looked over his shoulder and watched the two chained women continue to suck the man's cock. "This doesn't seem like you," she said finally. She couldn't picture Travers holding a whip or, God forbid, kneeling before a Dominatrix.

Travers smiled. "Brooks, we've been friends forever and I honestly believe there aren't too many people who know me better than you. But the boy you grew up with, the man you know at work, they're only parts of me. You've never seen me in the bedroom, sweetheart. You don't know what kind of lover I am any more than I know what kind you are."

"Sure you know, I just told you. I'm frigid." She meant her comment as a joke, but not even she could miss the pain lacing the last word.

Travers shook his head. "I don't believe that for a minute. A frigid woman doesn't beg to come to a sex club. She doesn't sit in a room surrounded by people acting out their lust-filled fantasies without even blinking twice."

Ginny laughed lightly. "You didn't see me when I stepped out of that bathroom. I've had a bit of time to adjust."

"A frigid woman doesn't come on her best friend's fingers by a campfire, screaming with ecstasy."

Ginny shuddered at the memory. Travers had never mentioned that night and sometimes she wondered if she'd dreamed it.

Travers reached up and touched the corner of her lips with his finger. "You aren't frigid—and I can prove it."

"How?"

"Unbutton your blouse."

Ginny frowned at his words before deciding he was teasing her. "Ha ha."

He didn't smile. He merely raised his eyebrows as if expecting her to obey his command.

"You're joking, right?"

He shook his head. She looked around at the other people in the room and chastised herself for thinking anyone would even glance their way. Looking back into Travers' face, she felt a devilish streak begin to emerge. What would he do if she took him up on his challenge?

Leaning back, she reached up and slowly began to slip the buttons from their holes, expecting him to stop her before she got too far. Travers didn't move a muscle, but his eyes followed her progress, and she was a bit unnerved by the desire she saw growing there. Once she finished, she froze, her hands lightly gripping the edges of the silky material, holding it together.

"Take it off," he whispered.

Again, Ginny glanced around the room.

"Don't look at them," Travers said harshly. "Keep your eyes on me, Ginny, and do as I say."

She sucked in a breath at the sound of her first name on his lips. She struggled to recall the last time he'd called her Ginny. Hell, when was the last time she'd called him Ryan?

Ryan. The sound of his name resounded in her mind like the pealing of a bell, and she was taken aback by the beauty of it.

"Ryan," she whispered, desperate to feel the weight of it on her lips.

"That's right," he answered. "Say my name, Ginny. Call me Ryan and understand what it means."

She frowned. "What it means?"

"It means you belong to me. Tonight, I'm your master."

Chapter Four

"Master?" Ginny repeated the word and wanted to laugh at the absurdity of his comment, but it didn't seem funny. Her affable, easygoing friend had turned into a dominant, commanding stranger. The worst part was, she was so turned-on by his demands she was too afraid to do anything that might remind him of who she really was and what they were to each other. They were friends—that was all they'd ever been. But tonight—Oh God, tonight—she wanted them to be so much more.

Ryan smiled at her question. "You belong to me, Ginny," he explained as if the fact he was going to take control of her body was a foregone conclusion. "Now take off that shirt."

Her hands began to tremble, but before her mind could process a single reason why this was wrong, she lifted them and slid the blouse off her shoulders. Ryan reached over and pulled it away from her. She was astounded by the fact she wasn't mortified to be sitting in a public place across from her best friend in merely a bra. Instead, for the first time tonight—hell, for the first time in her life—she felt like perhaps her world was realigning itself into the correct pattern.

What does that mean?

Ryan caressed her with his eyes, his gaze lingering on her breasts, and she felt her nipples harden in response. How could a single look make her feel so hot, so needy?

"You're beautiful," Ryan said, his gaze returning to her face. "You asked me why I was a member of this club." His words were spoken softly and Ginny leaned forward to hear him better. When his gaze dropped back to her cleavage, she wondered if his quiet tone wasn't premeditated.

"Perhaps," he said after a moment, "the better question to ask is why you wanted to come here so badly?"

Ginny considered his question and rather than avoid it, she decided to offer him the most honest response she had. "I was curious."

"Curious to see or curious to experience?" he asked.

She grinned ruefully. "I think the fact that I'm sitting topless in a room full of strangers should answer that question."

Ryan laughed softly and she savored the sound. She'd never noticed how sexy his laugh was or how amazingly handsome he was. He made her feel as if she was the only woman in the world and the power of that emotion took her breath away.

"How far will you go tonight, Ginny?"

She pondered his question and realized that the evening seemed to be built exclusively on truthfulness and on the exposing of deep, dark secrets. "With you?"

He nodded.

"As far as you'll take me. I trust you, Ryan."

Ryan sighed a breath of relief and struggled to believe this was truly happening. The night, thus far, had moved in painful slow motion, everything hazy and unreal until this moment when clarity had come. He felt as though he was seeing Ginny Brooks for the first time, in such crystal clear focus she was almost too stunning to look at.

Slowly, he rose and reached down for her hand. She placed it in his with a steadiness that confirmed the truth of her words. She did trust him. She would follow him wherever he led her. The enormity of that thought should have scared the shit out of him, but instead he felt lighter and happier than he had in years.

Turning, he walked with her to the opposite side of the room. He needed her to understand that with him, sex wouldn't be a game. It wouldn't be easy or familiar. He had dark needs that it suddenly seemed only Ginny could fulfill. He could hear her slight intakes of breath as they passed other couples and groups in the room.

The Voyeur Room was a place where club members could play or watch, depending upon their desires. There was a stage in the center of the room and at midnight, the planned entertainment would begin. Ryan glanced at his watch. He had more than enough time to play with his innocent friend before the show began.

He found what he sought after only a moment. Close to the stage was a large, overstuffed armchair. A soft light hung above it, giving the appearance of a spotlight. Ryan sat in the chair and gestured for Ginny to sit on his lap. He marveled at how easily she acquiesced to his demands. She curled into him, wrapping her arms loosely around his neck.

Bending forward, he claimed her lips in their first kiss since they were twelve years old. He'd wanted to taste her lush, lovely lips since he'd picked her up at her house. Dipping his tongue into her hot mouth, he explored and teased her. When they pulled apart, he could see the shock on her face as she felt him drag her bra straps over her arms and off. He'd taken advantage of her distraction during the kiss to unfasten the lacy scrap of material. He wanted to see if her nipples were as dark and large as they'd appeared when she'd removed her blouse. He wasn't disappointed.

She smiled when he reached down to cup her taut breast. That same smile vanished behind a moan when he pinched her nipple roughly.

"Oh, Ryan," she murmured as he repeated the action to her other tight nub.

"Stand up, Ginny, and face me."

It seemed to take her several seconds to clear away the haze of desire and process his words. He silently rejoiced. She was with him every step of the way in this, and he was blown away by her incredible sexuality. Jesus, had she really thought she was frigid?

She rose slowly, her hands hovering around her waist. He suspected she wanted to cover herself, and he was pleased to see her fighting the impulse. She was a born submissive and somehow, despite her lack of training, she knew better than to hide herself from him. Was it instinct? Ryan had no doubt she'd never traveled down the road of Domination and submission, yet she took to it as a baby bird takes to flight.

"Take off your skirt and panties, Ginny," he demanded, knowing this request was bound to test her limits. If she balked at being completely nude in a public place, what would he do? Ryan wished he could understand the genetic makeup inside him that wanted—hell, needed—this harder edge to sex. He'd given up trying to explain it and had instead embraced the needs, finding willing playmates and bed partners. However, this time, with Ginny, he was besieged by genuine hope and pure fear. He wanted her to want this. He needed her to need this.

She took a deep breath as Ryan held his and waited for her refusal. When she lifted her hands and began to undo the button at the top of her skirt, he fought against the urge to shout out his victory. If he'd had a football, he'd have slammed it in the end zone.

He watched as she slowly unfastened the zipper and shimmied the tight leather down her legs in a sensuous movement that have would put a belly dancer to shame. The sound of the leather lightly hitting the floor brought Ryan back to his senses, and he reached up to grip her hips, his eyes level with her pussy. Leaning forward, he breathed in her essence, getting drunk on her spicy scent. It took all the strength he possessed not to lean forward and lick the juices he could see gliding down her inner thighs.

"Turn around, Ginny. Face the room and sit on my lap."

For the first time, he sensed her hesitance. "You're beautiful and you're mine," he said. "Show them."

She seemed to gain confidence with his words and she turned slowly, lowering herself onto his lap. He wasted no time in moving her into the position he desired. Placing his hands on her knees, he pulled her legs apart, resting them over his own outstretched thighs. He felt her stiffen with the realization she was displaying her pussy for anyone in the room who cared to look.

He sensed her fighting the impulse to close her legs and he decided a bit of a reward was called for. Dragging his hands along the insides of her thighs, he touched her engorged clit with the tip of his finger, tapping it twice. She gasped and her head flew back, coming to rest against his shoulder. A fresh gush of juice flowed from her pussy and Ryan gathered it up, using the thick lubrication to ease his path as he rubbed his finger around her mons, toying with the tight entrance to her cunt.

She moaned again, louder, and Ryan glanced around the room. He could see that their play was gaining attention, their audience growing. He also knew Ginny was oblivious at this point to anything but his roaming fingers.

"Do you want more?" he whispered into her ear as she squirmed on his lap.

"Yes, please!"

"What do you want, Ginny? Tell me. Say the words."

Her breathing was harsh, labored, and Ryan marveled at the fact she seemed perilously close to coming.

"I want you."

"More specific," he demanded.

"Your fingers, your hand inside me."

"Inside your pussy?" he added for clarification, wanting her to become accustomed to the words.

"Inside my pussy," she repeated.

"You said my fingers, my hand. Which is it, Ginny? I have a feeling you don't really want my entire hand inside you. I doubt you've ever been fisted."

Ginny shivered and he knew she was shocked by his crude comment.

"Your fingers," she corrected, but her voice trembled as she spoke.

"You like the idea of taking my fist in your tight cunt, don't you?" As soon as he asked the question he realized it was true. He shook his head against the thought. There was no way he'd ever hurt her and a fisting definitely fell into the pain category, but the fact she was actually considering such an extreme concept gave him hope that she'd try other, safer things with him.

"I…I don't know," she admitted and again he was blown away by her honesty.

"Well, wildcat, you're going to have to make do with my fingers tonight." As he spoke, he dipped his hand lower, gathering up more moisture, stroking her clit several times before thrusting two fingers deep inside her pussy.

"Oh my God!" she cried out as he felt her inner muscles contract against his fingers. She came hard and loud and Ryan became aware of the fact that all activity in the room had ceased. He felt every eye in the place watching Ginny as she gyrated against his lap, lost in the throes of her orgasm.

When she began to settle, he whispered in her ear, “Open your eyes, Ginny. Look at them. They’re all watching you.” His fingers, still buried inside her, began to thrust again and he added a third to the first two. He felt her shock as she realized everyone in the room was watching the show they were putting on. He wondered if she balked at the thought—then he felt the slightest quivering begin in her pussy. Christ, she was going to come again. The idea of being watched clearly excited her as more moisture soaked his hand.

“You love this,” he said, not quite masking the amazement in his voice. “You love having them watch, don’t you?”

She nodded, but he wanted more.

“Say it,” he commanded harshly.

“I love it when they watch,” she admitted before turning her head slightly so it rested in the crook of her neck.

“Don’t hide your face, wildcat. They all think you’re beautiful too. Can’t you see it in their eyes? They all wish they were me.”

She turned and looked out into the room as Ryan increased the pace of his thrusting hand. She cried out, shoving her hips forward, silently begging for more. He obliged her by adding his thumb to the play. Countering each shove of his fingers in her pussy with a slow, hard rub on her clit, he tightened his grip on her as she shattered in his arms, her orgasm coming harder, louder, longer this time.

Her reactions left him burning, hurting, and he fought against the painfully hard erection threatening to rip the material of his dress slacks. He knew the show was scheduled to begin soon, but he found it impossible to care. They'd catch the next one.

He rose quickly—well aware that Ginny was still lost in the haze of her powerful orgasm—and carried her out of the room and down a long hallway. Placing her on her feet and wrapping an arm around her waist to steady her, he reached into his pocket to pull out a key.

"Where are we?" she whispered, her wits beginning to return.

"My room," he answered as he opened the door and led her inside.

The sound of the door closing and the lock clicking into place seemed to rouse her further still. "Where are my clothes?"

"An attendant will retrieve them and deliver them here."

"This is your room?" she asked.

"I'm a gold-card member," he reminded her. "That means I have my own room, decorated and maintained according to my personal preferences."

His answer piqued her interest and he watched her look around, taking in the room's furnishings. He wished he could read her mind, desperate to know what she was thinking as her gaze landed on some of the more unusual pieces.

"Oh," she murmured and he leaned back against the door, studying her face. He watched her eyes widen and her face go pale when they landed on the small cage in the corner of the room.

"I won't put you in the cage," he assured her quickly. "In fact, I can call for the attendant to take it away right now. I know you're claustrophobic."

Ginny turned and gave him a breathtaking smile. "I can't believe you remember that."

"Jesus, Ginny. I'm not likely to forget a thing like that. It was my fault you got locked up in that trunk in the first place."

"You didn't know the latch was broken and it was a pretty cool hide-and-seek spot."

Her words were easy and calm now, but Ryan had never forgotten the look on her face when he and Anderson had finally managed to free her from the old trunk he'd helped her hide in during a childhood game. She'd run straight into his arms and stayed there, shaking for ages. They'd never played hide-and-seek again, and Ginny's intense fear of tight, confined places was born.

"I'm not sure I know what all of this is for," she said, dragging him from his recollections as she walked over and ran her hand along the St. Andrew's cross dominating one wall of the room.

He grinned at her undeniable curiosity and again, he was amazed by the fact she wasn't freaking out and running away. The place must look like some sort of medieval torture chamber to her untutored eyes.

"I'm going to show you."

Her gaze returned to him, traveling down his body. She unconsciously bit her lower lip as she studied the all-too-prominent erection tenting the front of his pants.

"Don't be afraid, Ginny."

She looked up at his face, insulted by his words. "I'm not scared," she retorted and Ryan was reminded of her saying those words a thousand times as they were growing up. As the only girl in a gang of rough boys, she was constantly forced to prove herself.

"No, you're not," he agreed quickly. "But maybe you should be."

She smiled and shook her head. "Not with you, Ryan. Never."

Again, he was overwhelmed by her faith in him. She genuinely believed he would take care of her, make this good for her.

"Come here," he ordered, crooking his index finger at her.

She walked to him and attempted to wrap her arms around his neck. He grabbed her wrists roughly and pulled them to her sides.

"I won't make this easy for you, Ginny. I can't," he confessed, trying to give her one last opportunity to run, although at this point, he wasn't sure he'd let her make it through the door. There was no way he could let her go.

She gavc him a sassy grin and wiggled her eyebrows. "Travers, if I wanted easy, I sure as hell wouldn't be here with you."

He laughed at her familiar teasing. For nearly twenty years they'd fought like siblings, played with each other as children and worked side by side as colleagues. Tonight, they would add lovers to that list and the thought of it sobered him up.

"I thought I told you to call me Ryan," he said gruffly.

"Ryan," she whispered.

Chapter Five

"Go lay down on the bed," he commanded.

Although he wanted to try everything with her, he knew he'd never last long. She seemed to be shattering all of his hard-earned control. For the first time since he was a teenager, all he could think about was burying himself between a woman's sweet thighs and pounding his way into oblivion. There would be plenty of time for experimentation, for exploring after he'd relieved a bit of the pressure threatening to blow the end of his cock off. Christ, this wasn't like him. He was an experienced lover, a serious Dom, yet all he could think about right now was getting inside Ginny's body.

Ginny seemed to share his anxiousness as she quickly crossed the room to the luxurious king-sized bed that occupied one whole wall. She turned once she reached it and looked back at him.

"How do you want me?"

She was asking for more detailed instructions. Holy shit, where did this woman come from? His mind kept telling him to get it together. This was Brooks he was about to fuck. Problem was, the demands of his body were drowning out the logic in his brain, demanding that he touch her, kiss her, bind her, command her.

"Pull back the covers and lay down in the center."

She obeyed his orders as he slowly walked toward her. As he moved, he began to undress. Ginny's gaze never left his body, her eyes devouring every inch of the flesh he revealed to her bit by bit.

"Open your legs, Ginny," he said sharply. "Never close them."

She hastily did his bidding as he kicked off his shoes and quickly divested himself of his pants and boxers. Her eyes widened at the sight of him completely naked, and he wondered what she was thinking.

"You're on birth control?" he asked.

She nodded once, her gaze never wavering from his cock.

"I'm clean, Ginny," he continued, and she quickly looked up at his face. "I've never fucked a woman without a condom, but I won't wear one with you. If you don't want that, tell me now."

"I just want you, Ryan, with nothing between us."

He fought back a groan at her words and climbed on the bed, lying down beside her. Leaning down, he took her lips in a kiss that wiped away every wayward thought in his mind. He wanted her. He would have her. He remained over her, kissing her, running his fingers through her hair, savoring each whimper, each heated breath that passed from her lips. Hours seemed to go by, and yet he couldn't break the connection of their lips, their tongues. He could kiss her like this forever and never want for anything more in life.

"Ryan!" she cried, pulling back, her body restless, flushed, obviously ready for the next step.

"What do you want?" he asked, his voice rough with his own painful desires.

"You," she breathed.

He shook his head. "Not good enough. Tell me, Ginny. Tell me what. Tell me how."

"God!" she cried in frustration. She beat at his chest with her fists and he fought back a grin. It was apparent handing over all control in the bedroom was going to be a challenge for her.

Rather than acknowledge her comment, he simply bent forward and resumed his kissing. She succumbed to the first touch of his lips, grabbing his hair and roughly pulling him closer. He allowed her the brief moment of power before reaching up and disentangling her fingers.

Moving back, he looked into her eyes, studying her face, familiar and yet utterly new.

"You are so lovely," he murmured.

"Ryan," she answered breathlessly. "Make love to me."

Her words, so sweetly innocent, took him aback as he realized that was exactly what he planned to do. Every sexual experience in his life had been straightforward—albeit creative—fucking. He'd never made love to a woman, and he pondered the sadness of that fact before he looked at Ginny's beloved face and smiled. It seemed that he and this exquisite woman were destined to spend their lifetimes as each other's firsts. Her first kiss. Her first orgasm. His first real lover.

He rose over her, surrounding her with his body. She was so soft and warm, he pondered how he'd spent a lifetime in her presence never touching her. She welcomed him between her thighs, and he settled there before returning to the pleasure of just kissing her. He'd never spent much time on the art of kissing, of appreciating each warm breath, the sweet taste of a woman's tongue in his mouth, the delicacy of rubbing her soft lips with his. For a moment, he was swept back in time and he felt like they were twelve again, and the mystery of kissing was magical, new.

Despite Ryan's desire to savor her kisses, he could feel Ginny's impatience for more.

"Please, Ryan," she whimpered and he knew her body was in overdrive, desperate for him to come inside her.

Sitting back on his knees, he dragged his hands slowly down her lovely body, teasing her sensitive skin with his fingers. He cupped her breasts in his hands, bending down to steal one more taste, one more suck of her tempting nipple. She groaned as his lips enveloped the tight nub and he drew the peak more firmly into his mouth. His tongue darted out to circle the areola before his teeth gently nibbled.

"Oh my God," she whispered, and Ryan chuckled as her hips began frantically searching for him.

"Soon, wildcat," he murmured against her flesh and she hissed at him, moving against him faster, harder. Again, Ryan was reminded of the past. The memory of Ginny's wild thrusting against his fingers as he offered her that first taste of what it meant to have an orgasm.

His hand moved lower and her movements ceased. He sensed she was waiting for that first touch and he wondered how close to climaxing she was.

"You must never come without permission," he said firmly, and he tried not to smile when Ginny snorted in response.

"Not this time…please?" she asked, her voice near begging. "I'm so close, Ryan, so close."

"There is such a thing as anticipation," he said lightly.

"Are you kidding me?" Her voice climbed an entire octave as her question coincided perfectly with the first brush of his finger against her clit. Just a touch and then he moved on, rubbing her stomach, trying to calm her down. "I've been anticipating this for a lifetime. Please don't make me wait."

He felt the truth behind her words despite the shock he felt at hearing her confession. He dipped his fingers lower into her wet pussy and was rewarded with a loud whimper and a sea of wetness. She wasn't lying. She was more than ready to take him. And if he was being perfectly honest, he was ready for her. Hell, he was rock-hard and dying to take her.

Positioning the head of his cock at her opening, he glanced down at her face.

"The point of no return." As he spoke, he pushed inside her an inch or so awaiting her response, her confirmation that she wanted this as badly as he did.

She graced him with an impish grin. "No guts, no glory," she joked, and Ryan chuckled. She was and always would be his best friend, his best girl, the only woman he'd ever laughed with in bed.

Her smile quickly gave way to a moan as he pressed in—slowly but steadily. He was trying to read her body's response to his cock. She was too damn tight and if he hadn't known better, he'd have thought she was a virgin.

"Christ, Ginny," he gasped, pushing in a fraction more before retreating and returning.

"You're a bit bigger than my past—"

Ryan leaned down and stole the end of her sentence with his lips. He didn't want to hear about her old lovers. The thought of another man in her bed, in her body, made him see red, and those jealous feelings destroyed what little control he had over his body and its response to her. He pulled back until only the head of his cock remained inside before pure, pulsing instinct took over and, in one hard thrust, he seated himself to the hilt.

Ginny screamed at the intense impact, and he felt her inner muscles clawing at his painful erection, gripping and milking him hard as she came loudly. He clenched his jaw and attempted to ride out the storm of ecstasy. She may not be willing to hold back, but he fully intended to make this ride last. As she slowly came back to earth, he started his steady rhythm, not too hard, not too soft. He gave her time to recover. He fully intended to feel her heavenly orgasm against his flesh again. Christ, he intended to keep her coming all night long.

"Easy," he cooed in her ear as she started pushing back, trying to force her own tempo into his solid beat.

"So good," she panted. "So good…" Soon her words worked their way into the song playing in his own head, and Ryan found himself moving in time with her cry. He pushed faster, harder, as her words grew louder. "So good!" she yelled. "Oh my God, so good!"

On and on they moved in unison, his rough thrusts timed perfectly to the rearing of her hips and her words. Her hands joined in, scratching the notes onto his back as he buried his cock deeply, her womb fluttering against his tender flesh.

"Jesus," he muttered as she began to come again.

"Harder, Ryan, oh please, harder! So good…" she repeated and this time, he was defenseless against her attack. He fell headlong into his climax, his seed exploding from him in pulses that imitated her words.

"So good," he said, the words torn from his throat and—dear God—it felt like his heart as well.

So good, he thought, as the strength in his arms gave way. He fell to her side, gathering her in his embrace and holding her still-trembling body close to his.

So good.

Chapter Six

Ginny stirred when she felt a hand brush against her bare buttocks. For a moment, she struggled to remember where she was. When she recalled, she felt a grin cross her lips. Glancing at the clock on the bedside table, she could see it was only a little past one in the morning. She had been with Ryan less than four hours, and yet it seemed as if they'd lived a lifetime in just one evening. She still couldn't seem to make herself believe they were lying together in a bed, completely naked and recovering from some of the most mind-blowing sex she'd ever experienced.

"Don't plan on sleeping, wildcat. The night is young."

"I wouldn't dream of falling asleep." She turned to face him and was surprised by the stern look that had taken over his handsome face.

"I have to say, as far as subs go, you are probably the most ill-behaved one I've ever met. I seem to recall specifically telling you not to come without permission."

Ginny remembered his command and her immediate refusal. Shit, she would have exploded into a million pieces if she'd tried to hold back that orgasm.

"You're right," she agreed quietly, wondering where he planned to take them now. She'd sensed during their previous lovemaking that they were crossing a line she knew Ryan never crossed. He was a confirmed bachelor who restricted his affairs to this fantasy room he'd created away from his own personal lodgings, and he never, ever, let things get too heavy or too serious.

She shivered with anticipation when he rose from the bed, arms akimbo, and gave her a deeply masculine, wholly dominating look.

"Ginny, I think it's time you understood exactly who is in charge here."

Her stomach began to twitter with apprehension and excitement. Their earlier interlude in the bed had been sweet, but she knew this time Ryan fully intended to show her that different side of himself he'd alluded to in the Voyeur Room. In all their years of friendship, she would have said she knew every nuance, every deep, dark secret of this man. How could she have been so wrong?

"Are you familiar with any of the furniture in this room? Other than the bed, of course." He added the last so quickly she knew he must have read the playful reply hovering on her lips.

She sat up and looked around before pointing to the St. Andrew's cross. "I know that people are tied to that cross." She turned and gestured to the spanking bench. "And they're tied to that too."

"Do you know why?"

"For punishment?" she asked, her nerves overpowering her desire. What would Ryan do to punish her?

"There are many facets to BDSM, Ginny. Some people subscribe to all aspects, others to only a few."

"Which are you?"

Ryan grinned at her question. "In the bedroom, I'm the master and I expect you to understand that I will direct our play. I'm a firm believer in the concept of Domination and submission."

Ginny nodded and asked for clarification. "Only in the bedroom?"

"Only in the bedroom."

She could handle that. Hell, she loved the idea of handing all the decisions over to him. She had her hands full enough keeping control of her wayward engineers during the day. The idea of committing her body to the hands of a man she trusted was freeing, liberating in a way she couldn't quite explain, even to herself.

"Is that all?" she asked curiously.

Ryan must have read her enthusiasm. "I also enjoy bondage. Tying a woman up, having her at my mercy."

Ginny felt the reappearance of her arousal. Shit, she wasn't used to being wet, turned-on and horny for so long. The feeling was exhausting and exhilarating all at the same time.

"You like the idea of that," Ryan said, clearly reading her body's reaction.

Again she nodded, not trusting her voice. She was perilously close to begging him to take her again. She knew the request would be ignored this time. While she was overwhelmed by her continual need, Ryan had obviously regained control of his own sexual impulses and he wouldn't be led astray again.

"I'm not into the practices that are considered sadomasochistic. I'm not into extreme pain."

She tried to process his words, to understand and resign herself to the fact that this was Travers, her best friend, her boss, who was talking about tying her up.

"I don't think I'd like to be whipped," she admitted, as she recalled the chained women in the Voyeur Room. That thought led to another and she quickly added, "And I wouldn't like being pierced in any way."

"I would never dream of marring your perfect body in either of those ways," he reassured her. "But that doesn't mean I'd be averse to spanking your ass if I felt your behavior warranted it."

Ginny felt a fresh onslaught of arousal at his words, and she pressed her legs together in an attempt to stem the flow of juices from her pussy.

"Lay back down, Ginny, and put your hands above your head, crossed at the wrists." She sensed that was all the discussion Ryan intended to have regarding his sexual practices. No doubt anything else she learned tonight would be discovered firsthand.

She followed his command without hesitation. He placed a knee beside her bare hip and reached above her head. Looking up, she noticed him pulling on restraints that were attached to an eyehole on the headboard. She hadn't noticed them earlier.

"Have you ever been bound?" he asked.

"No," she whispered, unable to take her eyes off his hands as he reached for her wrists and began to secure the cushioned straps around them. The straps were padded and comfortable, while the feeling of helplessness was not. When he was finished, he tugged on the restraints firmly, silently driving home to her the futility of trying to escape.

His eyes were dark with arousal, and she fought to resist the growing need between her legs. She desperately wanted him to touch her clit. Again, she pressed her legs together, hoping to relieve some of the pressure building there, but Ryan quickly grabbed her knees, holding her legs open with a strength that caught her unaware.

"I warned you not to come without permission, Ginny. I suggest you obey me. Don't do anything I don't tell you to do."

"Ryan," she whispered. "I need..." She was too overwrought to complete the thought.

"I know what you need, wildcat. Now try to relax. I'm going to secure your legs."

His words sparked a flame inside her and she gave herself to him fully, wanting to know, to feel, to understand where this would all lead.

There were straps attached to the footboard of the bed as well, and Ginny wondered how she'd missed all this when they'd first entered the room. Of course, now that she thought about it, the bed had seemed to be the least intimidating piece of furniture. How foolish of her.

She fought against her rising climax as Ryan ran his hands along the arches of her feet. He'd yet to touch her in any truly sexual way, but she was so aroused by the feeling of the restraints holding her helpless to Ryan's will that she wasn't sure she'd be able to hold herself back.

When Ryan finished securing her ankles, he rose from the bed and looked down at her. Ginny fought to catch her breath as the feeling of being bound—naked and defenseless—seeped into her soul. She knew without a doubt she would hate this feeling if she were with any other man, but with Ryan, somehow it felt right, perfect.

Ryan rested his hand lightly on her stomach, the touch meant to comfort rather than stimulate. "How do you feel?"

"Fine," she confessed. "Better than fine."

She heard him laugh at her response and she smiled.

"I'm not going to give you a safe word, Ginny. If you want me to stop, tell me to and I will."

He knew her better than she knew herself, and she didn't have a doubt he would know if she became truly afraid.

"I'm not going to stop you," she said.

Ryan bent forward until his mouth rested at the shell of her ear. "Ginny, tonight is as much for you as it is for me. Don't do anything you aren't comfortable with just to please me."

Her heart fluttered at his kind words, but she knew in her heart she was going to love every little bit of experience Ryan exposed her to. She turned her head until her lips found his. She gave him a quick kiss. "I'm not going to stop you," she repeated.

Her words seemed to sink in and Ryan smiled. "Hold on, hot stuff. I've had a hankering to have you at my mercy ever since you were eighteen and gave your virginity to that dipshit Erik."

Ginny started to laugh but Ryan didn't give her the chance. Within seconds, his lips latched on to her breast, sucking, biting and teasing her nipple. Each caress, each touch took her breath away. She hadn't expected the feeling of helplessness to increase her pleasure to this extent, but it did.

He clearly wasn't lying about having her at his mercy, and apparently that so-called mercy was nonexistent as he continued to torment her breasts. She fought against the urge to beg him to fuck her, and she sensed she would never be able to stop herself from coming if he didn't ease up.

"Ryan, I can't stop, I can't—"

With a pop, Ryan released the nipple he was sucking and leaned forward. He gripped her head in his hands.

"If you come, Ginny, I'll flip you over on this bed and tie your knees to your elbows with that gorgeous ass of yours sticking up. I'll beat it, wildcat. I swear to God I will. Do you want that?"

For a brief, crazy moment, Ginny considered screaming, "Yes, please!"

For the first time, she fought against the restraints, desperate to ease the sudden throbbing between her legs. His words, his touches were driving her to the edge of pure insanity.

"Ryan," she gasped. "Help me."

"Be patient, wildcat."

"Fuck patient, Ryan! Fuck me!"

Ryan shook his head and seemed to stifle laughter. Ginny narrowed her eyes and decided it was a good thing he'd tied her up because the first thing she was going to do when he released her was kill him.

"If you keep trying to direct our course, you're not only going to find yourself in for a long night, you'll be gagged." Ryan reached toward the bedside table and pulled a device Ginny didn't recognize out of the drawer.

"Have you ever heard of a ball gag?" he asked.

Her eyes widened as she spied the rubber ball. Suddenly she was painfully aware of what the uncomfortable-looking harness would do. She shook her head.

"Will you behave?" He held it closer to her face and she nodded.

"Good," he said, tossing the gag aside. "I really want to hear your whimpers and moans." He moved back down her body as he spoke, bypassing her breasts, and Ginny gave him one of those whimpers he'd asked for.

Finally, she thought, as he moved toward her waist.

Unfortunately, he moved past her pussy until he was seated between her feet. Turning, he leaned over the footboard and reached down to rifle around in the trunk situated on the floor there. He pulled up a long length of rope, and Ginny began to squirm at the sight of it.

Crawling over her body, he straddled her hips with his strong thighs and again she was assaulted by the feeling of vulnerability his position created.

"You have the most amazing breasts," he murmured and she felt her taut nipples throb in response. She took a deep breath and savored his words as Ryan slowly and methodically began wrapping the rope around her chest in a complicated pattern. She had to arch her back, which was difficult with the restraints at her ankles and wrists, but he helped her, lifting her easily. The drag of the hemp beneath her served as its own form of sensual torture.

"The Japanese call sexual bondage Kinbaku. It's considered an art form and I've studied it a bit." As he spoke, his hands never stopped wrapping the hemp, using several overhand knots. When he finished, he leaned back to observe his work. He had wrapped her securely from waist to neck, her breasts lightly surrounded by the soft material, showcased by it.

"Oh my God," she said as she took in the intricate web-like pattern. "You're Spider-Man."

Ryan smiled. "And you're perfect," he whispered as he reached down to play with her nipples, leaning over and sucking each one tightly into his mouth. The feeling of being captured, caught and held in place for just this one man was so dazzling, she had to close her eyes against the wonder of it all.

Slowly he rose from the bed and again, Ginny was overwhelmed by the desire to call him back to her. He walked to the foot of the bed, untying first one ankle and then the other. She was surprised, not expecting their play to end so quickly. She started to close her legs but was halted by his harsh, “Don’t.”

He returned to the bed and reclaimed his place between her outstretched thighs, his hands moving along the rope at the edge of her waist before dipping his fingers down to her pussy.

“So wet,” he whispered. He pushed two fingers inside her, crooking them in such a way that he almost immediately found her G-spot.

“Oh God,” she cried, moving her hips toward his touch.

He continued to manipulate the sensitive place until Ginny was mindless, her orgasm starting to come.

“No,” he said as he removed his hand.

Ginny was too shocked by the abruptness of his retreat to speak. Every word that came to her mind at that moment was vulgar, furious, harsh. If she said what she was thinking, Ryan would no doubt continue to prolong her agony. She bit back her comments and sucked in lots of deep, deep breaths.

“Very good,” he said, and she struggled against the urge to scratch his eyes out. Not that she could have with her hands still secured above her head.

Ryan reached down and grasped her behind her knees, pulling them up until they rested on his shoulders. "I think you've earned a reward."

His words proved he knew how hard it had been for her to restrain herself, but when she felt his hot breath against her pussy, she was so glad she had.

"Yes," she hissed at the first touch of his tongue against her quivering mons. He pressed it firmly against her clit, and she fought not to shove her pussy against his talented lips. His tongue moved along the crease between her legs and pushed into her cunt. Over and over he fucked her with his tongue.

"Please, Ryan. Please," she begged.

He pulled out and said the words she'd been waiting a lifetime to hear. "Come, Ginny." He thrust his tongue back inside her and she exploded around it, screaming with the impact, the climax the strongest she'd ever had.

While she was still dazed from her orgasm, Ryan reached over to the bedside table and pulled out several items.

"How many things do you have in that drawer?" Ginny teased. Ryan looked back and smiled at the relaxed, happy look on her face.

"Boy Scout motto, wildcat. Always be prepared."

Ginny giggled. “Yeah, well, I know for a fact that you were never a Boy Scout.”

Ryan joined her laughter. “Can you blame me for that? They wouldn’t let my best friend join.”

“Well, at least we tried.”

He reached above her head to release her wrists, laughing over the memory of their little group of friends walking out of the Boy Scout meeting when the den mother refused to allow Ginny to stay. “I’m going to untie your arms, but the rest is staying unless you’re in pain.”

“I’m fine.”

He massaged her shoulders and arms for several moments while kissing her. “Better?” he asked.

“Perfect.”

“Roll over,” he ordered and Ginny complied.

“Get up on your knees and hold yourself open to me.” His directions seemed to give her pause and he grasped her hips, lifting her until her knees were directly under her. “Hold yourself open,” he repeated.

She slowly put her hands behind her and Ryan took them, placing them on the cheeks of her ass, showing her exactly what he wanted. “Pull them apart.”

She responded to his command, but he sensed her embarrassment at the act.

“I’m staking my claim, Ginny. Your ass is mine.”

She shivered at his words as he picked up the new tube of lubrication and still-packaged butt plug he'd retrieved from the drawer.

"You need to relax," he coaxed as he pushed the end of the lube into her dark opening and squeezed. She tried to pull away but he kept a firm hand on her back. "It will warm up in a minute."

He ran his fingers through her crease before using one finger to work the lube inside her. She hissed at the first touch of his finger breaching her, but she didn't try to escape again. Slowly he worked his finger in, one knuckle at a time until it was completely buried. Giving her a moment to adjust, he retreated and repeated the movement, increasing the pace until she began to move into his thrusts. He decided to push her further. He added a second finger to the sensual torture and rejoiced when she accepted it easily. He continued to finger-fuck her as she held herself open for him.

The image of Ginny in the wholly submissive position was one he felt certain he'd never forget. She was so beautiful, so trusting, so adventurous she took his breath away. She moaned as her ass muscles unexpectedly clenched his fingers, and he was shocked to feel her coming again. Christ, she was amazing.

As she came, he pulled his fingers out. He swiftly unwrapped the butt plug and slid it into place.

"Ryan?" she asked.

"Shhh. Just a little toy to stretch you a bit. Your ass is too tight for my cock and this will help."

Once he had the toy in place, he turned her over, enveloping her small body under his. He held himself up on his elbows and kissed her repeatedly. His cock was painfully rigid, but he couldn't seem to pull himself away from her sweet lips.

After what seemed like days, he drew away. "I want you to suck my cock," he said. "I want to come in your mouth and feel you swallow every drop of my seed."

She trembled at his words before nodding. "I want that too."

Propping her head on a pillow, he moved forward until he was straddling her chest. He nudged her lips with the head of his cock and was pleasantly surprised when she took him in without hesitation. She sucked on his flesh as if she was dying of thirst, and Ryan had to grip the sides of her head to slow her down. He fought against the urge that was telling him to give her what she was asking for. He desperately wanted to bury himself deep in her throat.

Her hands joined the game as she wrapped one around the base of his cock while the other squeezed his balls.

"That's right," he encouraged. "Suck it harder, Ginny."

She responded to his words and he fought to clear the red haze covering his vision. He would have to work hard to make this last. Her enthusiasm more than made up for her obvious lack of experience, and he couldn't help being pleased by the fact this act seemed unfamiliar to her. He was once again assaulted by an undeniable attack of jealousy. She belonged to him now. Her mouth, her cunt, her ass. The idea of any other man having her this way sent red-hot anger coursing through his body.

Fuck. What does that mean?

She gasped and he realized he was pulling her hair. He loosened his fingers and massaged her scalp in silent apology until her own grip on his balls tightened.

Shit. She seemed to be encouraging his roughness.

"Deeper, baby," he murmured, unable to stop himself from pushing her. She moved her mouth lower, taking in more of his cock. He brushed the back of her throat and her gag reflex triggered. He pulled out.

"Swallow the head," he instructed as he pushed back in. Again she seemed to fight his motion and her gaze searched his face. He pulled out and looked at her. She wasn't frightened, but she was definitely unsure if she could do as he was asking.

He paused for a moment. "We have all night, Ginny. I want you to swallow my cock, baby." He watched her eyes glaze over with the demand, and he was swept away by her innate submissiveness. He thrust into her mouth again and again as she gagged and struggled. He repeated the movement one more time and she shook her head.

He froze. "Do you want me to stop?"

Ginny seemed stunned by his question. She shook her head emphatically.

Not satisfied with her answer and determined not to frighten her, he repeated the question. Again, she shook her head adamantly and Ryan, appeased, surged into her mouth. She swallowed at the moment of impact and he found himself buried down her throat. The image of Ginny deep-throating his cock broke the restraints on his self-control, and he began to fuck her mouth in earnest. Ginny moved in tandem with him, milking the base of his cock with her hand and applying even more pressure to his balls.

"God dammit!" he cried as he felt the beginning of his orgasm. She swallowed deeply as he felt his semen hit the back of her throat.

When he'd released every drop, he slid out of her mouth and lay down beside her. He drew her into his arms, holding her tightly, with only one thought in his mind.

I'm never letting her go.

Chapter Seven

"Sorry, um…why are you here again?"

"Are you going to let me in or not, Allie?" Ginny, usually amused by her baby sister's smartass nature, was not in the mood.

"I'm still thinking about that. I mean it is pretty early on a Saturday and you arrived here in a taxicab. Obviously something is up and I'm thinking it might not be in my best interest to get involved."

"How 'bout I make this easy for you? Close that fucking door, take the chain off and open it again or I will squash you like the little bug you are."

"Well, that does seem to put things in perspective. Wait a minute."

Her sister shut the door and Ginny could hear her unhooking the security chain. A second later, the door opened and Ginny quickly walked in, past a confused Allie. Observing the terrycloth robe Allie wore and her mussed hair, it was obvious she'd woken her sister up.

"What time is it?" Ginny asked.

"How the hell should I know? You're the one up and about and beating on my damn door." Allie squinted toward the clock on her DVD player. "Aw hell, it's not even seven o'clock yet. What the hell is wrong with you? I didn't leave the dance club until nearly three a.m."

"I didn't want to go home," Ginny said as she sat down heavily on her sister's couch.

"Why the hell not? Hold on a second. What are you wearing? Is that a leather skirt?" Allie seemed to come awake at her appearance.

Ginny had hastily donned her clothing in Ryan's room upon waking and then she'd run straight here. Last night, she'd felt sexy. This morning, she just felt slutty. "Yes, it's leather."

"Where were you that you didn't want to go home from?"

"The Way Down Under Club," Ginny answered.

"The Way… What? Are you kidding me? You got an invite to that club and didn't call me? What kind of sister are you? You know I've been dying to see that place!"

"I didn't want to push my luck. Travers invited me for my birthday and I was afraid he'd change his mind if I made too big a deal of it." Even as she spoke Ryan's last name, she could taste the strangeness of it on her tongue. He would never be Travers to her again. The finality of that thought brought tears to her eyes.

"Are you crying?" Allie asked, sitting next to her on the couch. "What happened, sis? Did someone hurt you at the club? Where the hell was Travers?"

Allie's concerned voice and the consoling way she wrapped her arm around her opened the floodgates. It also brought home the fact no one would believe that she and Ryan had crossed the line from friends to lovers. Allie wouldn't understand that it was Ryan who had inadvertently hurt her simply by being too wonderful to be true. Ginny gave herself up to the tears as she thought about how Ryan had looked in bed this morning. He lay on his stomach, sprawled out, looking sexy as hell with his auburn hair tousled and covering his eyes. She turned toward her sister and cried, unable to say a single word.

Allie pulled her close and slowly rocked her. The movement reminded Ginny of their mother, and the thought brought forth another rush of tears. For several minutes, Allie said nothing beyond "hush" and "it's all right" and "don't cry".

Ginny struggled to pull herself together. She wasn't this type of woman. She never cried. The thought of being so weak jarred her from her miserable state, and she drew away from her sister.

"I'm sorry," she whispered, turning around to grab a tissue from the box Allie kept on an end table.

Allie smiled at her, though worry lined every part of the gesture. "I haven't seen you cry since grade school," she admitted. "I'm scared as shit right now. What happened, Ginny?"

Ginny tried to set her sister's mind at ease. "I'm fine. I shouldn't have carried on like that. I just—" Ginny sucked in a breath to hold back the sobs that threatened to come again. "I just made a huge mistake and I don't think there's any way to fix it."

"What mistake?" Allie asked.

"I had sex with R-Ryan last night," Ginny confessed, the words sticking in her throat as she spoke them.

"Ryan who?"

Ginny laughed at the unexpected question. Of course her sister wouldn't know who she was talking about—neither of them ever referred to Travers by his first name. Her sister's utterly perplexed face somehow managed to lighten Ginny's heavy heart.

"Travers," she explained.

Allie's jaw dropped and Ginny watched her sister struggle to form her next question—hell, her next word. "You? Travers? You? Sex? Oh my God!"

Ginny was a tad offended by Allie's total disbelief. "Well, I don't think it's that unfathomable."

"Ginny. Are you jerking my chain? What's the date?"

"Why?"

"It's gotta be April Fool's Day. You and Travers got together and decided to fuck with my head. That's it, isn't it?"

"Allie," Ginny said calmly. "I slept with Travers last night. We had sex—all night."

"Oh my God," her sister repeated, and this time Ginny realized the sentiment was correct.

"Yeah," she added. "Oh my God."

"How did this happen?" Allie asked.

"Oh you know, the usual way. What do you mean how did it happen?" Ginny felt her ragged nerves stretched even further under the pressure of her sister's utter astonishment.

"Ginny," her sister began impatiently. "You and Travers have been best friends since God was a baby. You've been drunk together, you've had sleepovers at each other's houses, you've gone on extended business trips and never, never have you stepped over the line of friendship. What happened last night?"

"It was my birthday," Ginny replied. Allie shook her head and raised her hands as if to say "so what?"

"Well, Liam said he had to work through the weekend, so we had to postpone our romantic getaway."

"Liam's a weenie," Allie interjected and Ginny smiled. Ryan had said basically the same thing and he'd been right.

"I agree."

"You do? Since when?" Allie asked.

"Since last night when I witnessed him wrapped around some slut at the Way Down Under Club."

Allie's face flushed with anger. "That motherfucker."

"Amen, but that's not really the point here, is it?"

Allie looked at her thoughtfully. "I don't know. Maybe that is the point. Travers invites you to the club, you see your boyfriend doing the nasty with some whore, so you hop into bed with someone convenient. If I know Travers, he was as pissed off as you at the sight of Liam and he tried to comfort you, right?"

"Sort of," Ginny said. She didn't like thinking of Ryan as a convenience or a consolation prize. What they'd done together far surpassed mere consoling or a rebound response on her part.

"I'm not really surprised you ended up in bed with Travers," Allie added so confidently Ginny wasn't sure how to respond.

"Really? Why not?"

"Because he's a little crazy when it comes you. Always has been."

Ginny shook her head, unsure she'd heard her sister correctly. "Wait a minute. What do you mean 'crazy'?"

"It's always the same thing whenever you're around him. He has one eye on whatever is happening in the room and one eye on you."

"Allie, I have no idea what you're talking about." Could her sister's words be true? Had Ryan been protecting her all these years? Was his response last night not one of desire, but instead of comfort? The thought of Ryan sleeping with her merely out of pity made her stomach lurch with nausea.

"Anderson's even joked about it a few times. Says Travers never sees any other woman when you're in the room. Says his friend's 'knight in shining armor' attitude only shines for you."

"Anderson said that?" Ginny asked. Suddenly Allie's words took on a different meaning. Could it be possible that Ryan had been interested in her all of these years?

"Yep, Anderson and I have had several conversations about you and Travers. I have a feeling he won't be so surprised when he hears the two of you finally did the dirty between the sheets."

Ginny had to laugh at Allie's use of Anderson's expression. The man had never used the word "sex" in his life. He only ever said people did the "dirty". The childish expression drove Taylor nuts, which—Ginny was certain—was why Anderson continued to use it.

"Yeah, well, Travers and I really had no business doing the 'dirty' or having sex."

“Was it that bad?” Allie asked.

“Holy hell, no! It was great, amazing, fucking out of this world.”

Allie looked confused. “Then what’s the problem?”

“The problem is Ry— I mean Travers and I are friends. Sex screws up friendships. Everybody knows that.”

Allie shrugged, unconcerned. “So you hit the sheets and had hot sex together one night. So what? Good for you and good for Travers. There’s no hard and fast rule that says you can’t be friends anymore. What did Travers say this morning?”

Ginny turned her head toward the window, unsure how to answer.

“Aw shit,” her sister murmured. “You didn’t stick around, did you?”

Refusing to meet what she was sure was a condescending look from her baby sister, Ginny watched as the sun rose more fully in the sky, wondering if Ryan was awake yet. “There didn’t seem to be much point in sticking around. It’s not like Ryan— I mean Travers said anything about us having a future or anything. Last night was just a bit of experimenting between friends.”

“What kind of experimenting?” Allie asked, and Ginny realized her sister had just remembered the part about the sex club.

"The kind you're too young to hear about," she replied in her haughtiest older sibling tone.

"Bullshit," Allie answered. "You can go ahead and climb down off that high horse, sister dear, because you and I both know my 'experience' in that arena far surpasses yours."

Ginny bit her lip but refused to admit her sister's words were true. Allie had been a free spirit from the crib, and Ginny didn't even want to begin to ponder some of the "experiences" her sister had enjoyed.

"Fine, let's just say we were in a sex club and leave it at that. I think I'll just let your twisted mind fill in the blanks."

"Sis, you do not want me to fill in the blanks," Allie teased.

"Actually, I think I do." Ginny tried to ignore the heat she felt creeping up her face and the wide-eyed expression her sister gave her.

"Holy hell, what did you two do?"

"That's not really important, is it?" Ginny asked.

"No, what's important is the fact that you ran like a big fat chicken."

"I didn't run," Ginny protested. "I merely got out of bed, got dressed and grabbed a cab. Is it my fault he didn't wake up?" She silently thanked God that Ryan had taken out the butt plug and untied the rope binding her before they fell asleep. She'd been in such a hurry to flee this morning, she wasn't sure she would have taken the time. She could just imagine her sister's face if she'd showed up here walking funny and with a mile and a half of hemp twisted under her shirt.

Allie rolled her eyes. "What a lame excuse! I'll bet you were quiet as a mouse the whole time you were making your escape. Why the hell did you run?"

Ginny took a deep breath and considered the question. Truth be told, the same one had been haunting her since she'd asked the doorman to call the taxi for her. "I just didn't want to have to endure his 'morning after' routine."

Allie narrowed her eyes. "What are you talking about?"

"Travers and I have been friends for a very long time. I think I've heard every ridiculous excuse he's ever made to escape after a roll in the hay with some woman. I didn't want to be yet another victim of his fuck-and-run routine. I didn't want to be left lying in that bed, naked and alone."

"So you made sure he was naked and alone," Allie said.

"You think I was wrong?"

"I think you owed it to your best friend to give him the benefit of the doubt. Regardless of his past relationships, you are different, and I think you should have stayed. My sister, the one I've spent my entire life emulating, would have stuck around."

Ginny quickly swiped away a wayward tear. "I couldn't," she answered, her voice breaking on the words.

"Why not?" Allie asked, grasping Ginny's hand tightly between her own.

"Because I couldn't have taken it if he'd walked out. Dammit, Allie! I love Ryan."

"Of course you do. He's your best—"

"No," Ginny interrupted. "I'm in love with him. I think I always have been."

Allie's face gentled into compassion incarnate. "Oh, Gin. That's exactly why you should have stayed."

* * *

Ginny tried to concentrate on Anderson and Taylor's story about their weekend, giving them a fake laugh every few minutes so they'd think she was listening, but she repeatedly felt her eyes roaming toward the front door. How would Ryan— Crap! Travers—she really needed to remember to call him Travers—react when he got to work?

She was convinced now that Allie had been right and she'd been wrong to sneak out the way she had. She should have stayed, let the scene play out. If she had, she wouldn't be facing this awkward situation now—in front of two unsuspecting friends. Somehow the idea of playing the tongue-tied, "so what do we do now" game with Travers had seemed too hard to face at the time. Shit, she'd give anything to go back in time and get this first conversation over with…in privacy.

He'd given her a hell of a birthday, but she wondered if—for him—that's all it was. Travers was a love-'em-and-leave-'em kind of guy. She'd wanted to experience a night in a sex club, and he'd given her that experience and then some. Never once during the night had he mentioned what would happen the next day and, as Ginny relived the night over and over in her mind during the weekend, she'd convinced herself that could only mean that there wasn't going to be a next day. Travers didn't know her feelings had changed and, even if it killed her to keep the secret, she sure wasn't going to drop a bombshell like love down in the middle of their friendship. The foundation of their whole relationship, after Friday night's affair, was bound to be shaky enough as it was.

Despite Allie's insistence that she face her fears, she'd hidden out at her sister's townhouse all weekend, claiming she'd needed time to think and clear her thoughts. She'd actually thought perhaps the distance would shake loose her notion of being in love with Ryan.

Fat chance.

When she'd returned to her own home late last night and checked her answering machine, she'd been shocked to find Travers had left fifteen messages, each one a bit more tense and angry than the last. She wasn't sure why she was surprised by the number. He'd called Allie's place twice, but when her sister's caller ID flashed Travers' name, Ginny had forbidden her to answer. To make matters worse, she'd left her cell phone in his car the night he'd driven her to the club.

"So that's when security showed up," Anderson said, and Ginny offered a faint laugh although she didn't have a clue what he was talking about.

The ringing of the bell over the front door alerted her to Travers' arrival. Anderson looked at the clock on the wall with astonishment.

"What the hell? Travers, I think this is the first day you've ever shown up early to work since we opened the firm. What's the occasion?"

Travers ignored Anderson and looked straight at her. She sensed him holding back his anger, the look in his eyes unreadable, and her stomach fluttered in fear. Maybe with her thoughtless, selfish retreat, she had killed the friendship.

Taylor leaned back in the chair across from her desk. "Jesus, Anderson. I think we stepped into a black hole or something. Travers is early, Brooks is in a skirt. Do you think hell froze over while we were out of town?"

Travers seemed to process the comment that she was wearing a skirt, while Taylor kept speaking. "You're just in time to hear about our weekend."

Travers nodded, his eyes still glued to her face. "Great," he said stiffly. "Did you have a nice weekend, Brooks?"

She swallowed heavily and tried to put on a happy face. The last thing she wanted right now was a bunch of questions from Anderson and Taylor if they became suspicious. "It was fine. I decided to hang out at my sister's for the weekend since Liam couldn't make it for our trip out of town."

"I tried to call," he stated, his voice rife with annoyance.

"I left my cell phone in your car Friday night."

"I noticed." He pulled it out of his pocket and placed it none too gently on her desk.

"Hey, that's right. How was your trip to the sex club, Brooks?" Anderson asked.

"It was fine." She was aware she was repeating herself with simple, stupid answers, but she was having a difficult time getting her brain to function.

"Bet it was a bit of a disappointment, eh?" Taylor asked, clueing Ginny in to the fact that her friends were well aware of Travers' original intentions of limiting her tour to the bar.

"No, not really," she answered lamely. Frantically searching for a way out of the uncomfortable conversation, she added with a lighthearted giggle, "But finish your story first."

Ryan headed for his office, and Ginny tried to ignore the undeniable anger in his gaze. "I have work to do," he announced shortly. "I'll have to hear all the gory details later." With that, he walked into his office and slammed the door.

"What the hell is his problem?" Taylor wondered aloud.

Ginny shrugged, pressing a fist against the growing pain in her stomach. For a moment, she thought he'd seemed more hurt than angry. Christ, she'd screwed up royally. Standing, she said, "Excuse me, guys," and walked into Ryan's office before she could talk herself out of it.

She heard Taylor mutter, "What the hell is her problem?" as she left the room.

Ryan looked up in surprise when she shut his office door behind her.

"I'm sorry," she said quickly. "I was a gigantic ass and I'm so, so sorry."

Ryan gave her a lopsided, familiar grin, and she felt the aching in her heart begin to fade. "Why did you run away?" he asked.

"I just didn't want to put either one of us through that weird morning-after crap."

His eyes narrowed at her comment. "That's funny, Brooks. My plans for the morning after included more sex and then a big breakfast."

She stifled a groan at the thought of more sex with Ryan. She'd been struggling to push down her arousal since he'd walked through the door. Apparently the smell of his shower gel was going to be a trigger for her orgasms for years to come, and the thought of never being with him again left her struggling to get air into her lungs.

She tried to think of a joke, some way to get them back to their usual casual, fun banter, but nothing would come.

"Well, I just wanted to say I was sorry and to thank you for a great birthday. I should probably get back to work."

"Stop," he said as she turned and reached for the doorknob.

"Travers, we really don't have to talk about this. I mean it was just one night. We're still friends. Nothing's changed."

"Come here, Ginny." His voice was firm and the moment she heard her name on his lips, she felt her pussy flood with her body's juices.

She didn't move, too confused, too aroused.

"I'm not going to repeat myself," he said, his voice deep and commanding. The sound of it elicited the same response it had on Friday night. She turned and walked to his desk. He was sitting in his large leather office chair, but he had pushed it back a bit. She thought perhaps he was going to rise but he stayed seated.

"Come around the desk and stand here." He pointed to a spot between his thighs.

The thought that he might actually want to continue their affair terrified and delighted her at the same time. She moved slowly, trying frantically to read his face, to find some clue as to what he was thinking.

When she reached her destination, he put his hands on her hips, holding her in place as he gazed up into her face.

"Why are you wearing a skirt?" he asked.

She blushed, uncertain how to respond. Shrugging, she decided to go with the truth. "I knew you'd be pissed off at me for running away this weekend. I thought maybe this would soften you up."

Ryan laughed at her answer. "Yeah? Well, it worked. Sort of. Turn around and face the desk, Ginny."

She turned and caught sight of the office door. She wasn't sure what he intended, but just in case, she quickly said, "I didn't lock the door."

"An oversight on your part. One I expect you won't make again in the future. Bend over." His hand touched the top of her back and he firmly pushed her forward.

"Travers—" she began, but he stood and leaned over her quickly, roughly covering her body with his.

"If you call me Travers again, I won't be held responsible for my actions." His voice was angry, hard.

"I'm s-sorry, Ryan," she answered breathlessly when he didn't move.

Seemingly appeased by her apology, he stood up and gripped the hem of her skirt. He pulled it up to her waist and sighed as if annoyed. "You're wearing panties," he stated.

"Of course I am," Ginny answered matter-of-factly and he chuckled.

"Stand up, take them off and give them to me. Then return to this position."

She obeyed his request, her gaze continually straying to the door. What would Anderson and Taylor say if they walked in and found her bent over Ryan's desk with her bare ass in the air?

Ryan seemed to read her thoughts. "They could come in, you know. At any minute, they could open that door and see you like this. What would they say? What do you think they would do?"

Ginny's heart began to race with excitement at his words, and her breath was coming out in gasping pants.

"Would you let them watch us, Ginny?"

She shivered at the thought of Anderson and Taylor sitting on the couch, watching Ryan take her from behind.

"Would you let them join in?"

His question startled her and she held her breath as she thought about it. Would she? No, she thought. No, she wouldn't. She didn't want any man to touch her but Ryan. She shook her head in response.

"Good," he murmured, leaning forward to whisper in her ear. "I'd kill any man who touched you, friend or not."

She whimpered at his words, the power, the sureness behind them, thrilling her to the bottom of her soul.

"Now—let's talk about your punishment."

She tried to push up at the word, but Ryan held her firmly against the desk's surface.

"You were wrong to run, Ginny, but that I can forgive. It was an impulsive move and you are nothing if not impulsive. It's your nature, your personality. What I can't forgive is that you hid from me all weekend. You aren't a coward but you acted like one. After nearly twenty years of friendship, you should have come to me, talked to me. I thought you trusted me."

"I do," she whispered, tears filling her eyes. She was ashamed of herself. Every word Ryan spoke was the truth and she had been terribly wrong to avoid him. To avoid this.

"Why, Ginny? Why did you hide from me? Were you afraid of me? Did I scare you? Hurt you?"

Ginny's heart broke at the fear in his voice. Dear God, he thought she'd run away because she was afraid of him? That he'd caused her pain? "Oh no, Ryan," she answered hastily. "You didn't hurt me at all. I loved every minute of Friday night."

She sensed the tenseness she'd seen and felt in his body since he had arrived at work suddenly vanish. "Then what made you hide?"

"I was afraid it was a one-night stand, a birthday fuck, and that you wouldn't want to be with me again. I thought if I created some distance, maybe I wouldn't want you to touch me so badly. Maybe I could come to work today and not sit at my desk all day dreaming about every wicked thing I want your hands to do to me."

Ryan was silent and she wished she were looking at him. Wished she could see his face and read his thoughts. When the silence continued, dragged on for too long, she started to push up again.

She was firmly held in place. "If you attempt to stand again without permission, I'll beat your ass with that ruler until you can't sit at your desk at all."

Ginny's eyes landed on the ruler lying next to her head, and she squeezed her thighs together at the thought. Ryan must have sensed her excitement at his threat.

"Jesus," he sighed. "You've been right through that wall all these years."

She wasn't sure what he meant, but she didn't have time to ponder it as she felt him reach down. From the corner of her eye, she could see him digging through his briefcase.

She jerked slightly when she felt him lay several items on her back.

"Ryan?"

"Hush," he said. "I'm afraid dreaming about my hands is all you're going to be allowed to do today. You were wrong to hide, Ginny, but perhaps more so, you were wrong to assume what you and I did on Friday night was a one-night stand. Hopefully today will help you realize what a mistake it is for you to fail to communicate with me. Think about the fun we could've had this weekend if you'd merely stuck around Saturday morning to talk to me about your fears."

Ginny squirmed uncomfortably, wondering what his intentions were. His fingers wiped those thoughts away as he reached down and drove one deeply inside her pussy.

"Oh yes," she breathed.

He thrust in and out with the single finger several times, and Ginny struggled not to beg him to add another.

She cursed under her breath when he removed the finger completely and Ryan tsked at her language.

"Careful, Ginny," he warned. "Everything you do and say now will only prolong your punishment."

What the hell did that mean? She was panting and so desperate to come she couldn't stand it. She'd long ago given up worrying about the unlocked door and Anderson and Taylor.

She felt cold lubrication hit her ass, and she gripped the edge of the desk to stop from pushing herself up. Ryan was the first man to ever play with her ass and while the idea still scared her a bit, she couldn't deny the pleasure she felt in the dark act.

"You've wasted our time. Spent the weekend hiding from me when we could have been playing, experimenting, coming. Today, you're going to have to suffer the way I suffered all weekend." As he spoke, he worked the lubrication into her ass with one finger, and Ginny was helpless to stop herself from pushing back against it.

"Uh, uh, uh," he admonished. "None of that for you." He pulled his finger out and again, Ginny felt her temper rise. She was perilously close to an orgasm, yet Ryan refused to give her release.

"Please," she whispered.

"Go ahead and beg. It won't do you any good. I begged you to call me back—all weekend—and you left me hanging. Now it's your turn."

She groaned as he inserted a small vibrator into her cunt. He turned it on low and Ginny felt her inner muscles quiver against it. While the vibrations felt good, the device was too tiny to push her over the edge. A moment later, she felt the tip of something at her anus.

"I thought we'd try the next size up," Ryan said as he slowly worked the butt plug into her ass. "Push against it, Ginny. Don't fight it. It's nowhere near as big as me and I'm definitely going to start fucking that ass of yours soon."

Ginny pressed her forehead against his desk and gave herself up to the tight, slight burning sensation caused by the plug as Ryan worked it in. When it was fully seated, he gently gripped her elbow.

"Stand up."

Was he kidding? She could barely think, let alone move. Her mind was solely focused on the vibrator and the butt plug. While she felt very full and utterly turned-on, she knew neither device was going to give her the climax she was beginning to suspect she'd commit murder to achieve.

He helped her stand upright before stealthily tucking her panties into a desk drawer.

"You can't leave me like this," she said, gripping his arms for support when he lowered her skirt.

"Why not? You left me in exactly this condition all weekend. Now I want you to go back to your desk and get to work. You are not allowed to touch yourself and you're not allowed to come. I'll know if you do."

She stared at him as if he'd lost his mind. She wanted to protest his cruelty, but her mind couldn't get beyond his words. You left me in this condition all weekend.

Turning, she walked back toward the front room and her desk.

"Oh, and, Ginny," he said as she reached for the doorknob, "leave the door open."

Chapter Eight

Ryan remained in his office all morning, refusing Taylor and Anderson's invitation to lunch. Of course Ginny had declined as well, no doubt unable to walk given the toys he'd left filling her pussy and ass. She'd been squirming like a child in church, and he'd taken far too much pleasure out of watching her breathing accelerate and her cheeks flush every time he adjusted the speed on the vibrator. He patted the remote in his pocket and wondered if it was time to give her another jolt.

He tried to feel guilty for torturing her so, but he'd spent the entire weekend out of his head with worry only to come into work this morning to find her hanging out with Anderson and Taylor and chatting and laughing as if she didn't have a care in the world. Her apology and explanation, while sweet, didn't do much to soothe his ragged temper, and he wondered where in the hell she'd come up with the idea that he'd intended their Friday night liaison to be nothing more than a fucking birthday present.

He heard Anderson and Taylor call out their goodbyes and listened as Ginny reminded them about their afternoon meeting. Neither man intended to return to the office for the day. Ryan grinned at the thought and wondered if Ginny would make some excuse to try to leave as well. Instead, the office phone rang and he heard her answer it as the front door closed behind his partners.

They were alone. Ryan grinned and decided it was time for the punishment to end. Fact of the matter was, watching her fight her arousal all morning had his cock as stiff as a baseball bat and if he didn't find his own release soon, he was afraid the thing would disintegrate under the pressure.

Unfortunately, he knew it was more important that she learn her lesson, so he'd suffered right alongside her. His girl had scared the hell out of him when he'd woken up alone in bed on Saturday, unable to find her. He'd torn through nearly the entire club before the doorman saw him and mentioned calling a cab for his date. He was determined to make damn sure she understood two things before she left this office today—number one, she would never run from his bed again and number two, she belonged to him.

As he glanced out his office door, he saw that Ginny had her back turned to him and he sensed she was trying to keep her conversation private. He rose and walked toward her.

"Liam," she said. "I'm not interested in seeing you tonight. I told you this morning, it's over." She paused, no doubt listening to the asshole's excuses. "No," she answered. "I really don't feel like going into my reasons why. Not over the phone and certainly not in person."

She wasn't going to tell him about catching him red-handed at the club. Ryan watched as she rubbed her hand against the back of her neck, and he could see the weariness of the gesture as Liam apparently continued to plead his case on the other end of the line.

"Okay, fine! I'll tell you why. Four words, Liam—Way Down Under Club."

Ryan grinned at the cold tone in her voice.

"What do you mean what was I doing there? That's hardly the point, is it? You're a two-timing jerk and I—" Apparently Liam had interrupted.

"No, I don't want to go to dinner, you dumbass!" she answered.

Ryan felt his temper flare at the fact Liam obviously seemed far more interested in Ginny now that he knew she'd gone to a sex club. Hell, he was steamed she was even talking to the little prick while she had his toys buried inside her.

"Hang up the phone," he commanded as Ginny jumped slightly at the sound of his voice right behind her. She turned slowly, the phone still at her ear.

"No, Liam," she whispered.

"Hang it up, Ginny," he repeated.

When she failed to respond to his demand, he walked behind her desk, picked up the base of the phone and ripped it from the wall.

Ginny exploded. "What the hell did you do that for? Do you know how much it's going to cost to fix that? Shit, Travers, that phone is a big part of this firm's livelihood!" No doubt her temper was as ragged as his. They'd both spent the last few hours on the verge of an orgasm with no hope of release.

"Get in my office!" he shouted. "Now! And if I hear the name Travers cross your lips one more time today, I swear to God I'll beat your ass."

His heated words and threat didn't seem to penetrate her consciousness. "Listen, Travers," she said, dragging out the name. "I don't appreciate being ordered around like this! The bedroom is one thing, but this is my job. You can't stuff me full of vibrators and plugs and expect me to get a damn thing done around here!"

"Get. In. The. Office." He spoke the words through gritted teeth and at last, Ginny's sense of self-preservation seemed to seep through to her sex-starved mind.

She walked slowly toward his office but Ryan wasn't in the mood to be kept waiting. He grabbed her hand and dragged her behind him, slamming his office door so hard that two pictures fell off the wall.

As he turned to face her, he watched as she opened her mouth to lambaste him. Unwilling to hear any more of her angry comments, he pulled her toward him and kissed her—hard. Each time he broke away she attempted to speak, and he silenced her again with his lips. Over and over, they fought a battle of wills until he finally felt her body relax against his. Only then did he gentle the kiss and wrap his arms around her as she curved her soft body into his hard one.

"Ryan," she whispered when he pulled away.

"That's right. I'm Ryan," he murmured, running his tongue along her lower lip. "Now take that damn skirt off."

When she failed to move quickly enough, he reached back and smacked her bottom.

"Ouch!" she cried. Ryan silently kicked himself. He'd forgotten about the butt plug. Dammit if Ginny Brooks wasn't pushing every hot button in him.

He tried to take a calming breath as he watched her reach up to unbutton her skirt. His gaze landed on her breasts, and he could clearly see the tight nub of her nipples poking through the material of her blouse.

Jesus, she was turned-on by his spanking. He should have realized. After everything they'd done Friday night, he knew her taste for sexual adventure more than matched his.

He reached back and spanked her again. "Hurry up," he commanded. This time she groaned and he felt his control snap. He reached over and ripped her blouse down the middle, buttons flying in every direction.

"Are you crazy?" she asked. "What's gotten into you?"

"Do you want a fucking list? You. You've gotten into me, and now that you're there I expect you to do as you're told. Go back to my desk and assume the position you were in earlier." The position that had driven him out of his mind for hours. The vision of her bare ass displayed before him had taunted him, and now he was about to finish what he'd wanted to do to her this morning.

Without further comment, she walked to his desk, calmly pushed a few things aside and leaned over it.

"Fuck, you're gorgeous," he said as he walked up behind her and ran his hand across her soft ass, his fingers toying with the end of the butt plug.

He dipped his hand into the crease, finding the opening to her pussy. Her juices instantly coated his fingers. "Spread your legs," he demanded, pushing her feet apart with his own. She obliged and he slowly pulled the vibrator out. She shoved back as if she wanted to keep it inside her, and Ryan threw it across the room jealously.

Unable to fight the need to claim her, he thrust three fingers roughly in and out of her pussy.

"Oh God!" she cried, her inner muscles quivering against his unrelenting invasion.

Quickly he pulled his fingers out and landed five hard spanks against her ass. He knew each blow was jarring the butt plug, but her cries and pleas for more let him know she liked the roughness of his hand. The flesh of her ass heated and turned a deep shade of red.

Rather than retreat, she began to push back against him, silently begging for more. Ryan wholeheartedly obliged, peppering her buttocks and thighs with firm slaps. Ginny's groans grew louder and twice his hand slipped in the hot fluid flowing from her pussy, down her legs.

"More!" she cried and Ryan could hear in her voice how close she was to the end. Unwilling to let her forget this was a punishment, he stopped. Ginny jerked up from the desk angrily, but Ryan refused to give in. He pushed her to her knees in front of him, hastily unfastening his pants.

"You forget, wildcat. You're being punished. You don't come until I do." As he spoke, he pulled out his rock-hard flesh and gripped her hair. She reached up to grasp his cock, but he tapped her cheek lightly. "No, no hands. Just your mouth."

Ginny's brown eyes went black with arousal and Ryan could see her fighting against her own release. She might not like the punishment, but she would obey. God, he was never letting her go. She was his.

The first touch of her lips against his cock drove all thoughts of possession from his mind, and he gave himself up to her talented mouth. She'd remembered her lessons from Friday night well and swallowed the head of his cock on the third thrust. Ryan felt the tenuous grip he had on his control slip and he pulled her hair—hard. Forcing her to take more of him. Hell, forcing her to take all of him. On and on he drove into her mouth. Ginny whimpered against him but he couldn't stop. Not 'til she'd taken his seed, his love, everything he had to give.

He shouted with his climax and was amazed to realize Ginny was coming too. Her body trembled as she fought to control her orgasm while drinking down his come. All the strength in his body left him and he fell to his knees before her. Reaching up, he gently massaged her head, consumed by guilt for his too-rough hold. An apology hovered on his lips but before he could speak, Ginny leaned up and kissed him so sweetly he couldn't breathe. His heart seemed to burst from the onslaught of unfamiliar emotions attacking his system.

Slowly, he pushed her onto her back on the rug, moving over her. He positioned his rejuvenating cock inside her welcoming body, thrusting gently. She was tight, the butt plug still firmly encased in her ass. When he'd seated his cock to the hilt, he stopped and looked into her beloved face.

"Okay?" he whispered, afraid of hurting her. She was so tiny, so tight, and despite his body's demands that he take all of her, claim every part of her body as his own, his conscience screamed that he protect her, cherish her.

"Okay," she replied with a soft smile.

In and out he pushed, his mind silently chanting words he didn't comprehend until they both succumbed to the sweetest of orgasms. It wasn't until she reached over and placed her small hand on his rapidly beating heart that he recalled the words that had been echoing through his brain as he'd made love to her.

Love you, love you, love you…

* * *

Ryan opened his eyes in the dimly lit room and looked straight into the pissed-off gaze of Charlie Anderson. He wondered for a moment why his friend was so angry—until he felt Ginny's hand move against his chest.

Anderson jerked his thumb toward the door, indicating for Ryan to follow. Carefully, he disentangled himself from Ginny's slumbering form and covered her nude body with his shirt. He tried to still the green-eyed monster that was clawing in anger at the thought of Anderson seeing her naked.

Glancing out the window, he saw night had fallen. He and Ginny had done nothing but doze between sexcapades all afternoon before finally falling asleep together on the sofa in his office.

He'd taken her doggy style across the desk. She'd straddled his lap and ridden him while he sat in his office chair. They'd performed a sixty-nine on the floor. His entire office was filled with the scents of their combined juices, and the place looked like a tornado had torn through it. Only a fool would fail to realize what had taken place here all day and unfortunately, Charlie Anderson was nobody's fool. Ryan took a deep breath and threw on his pants.

He walked out into the main office, shutting the door behind him, unwilling to disturb Ginny with what was sure to turn into a brawl. He couldn't remember the last time he'd seen Anderson so angry.

His friend turned as soon as he emerged from the office, but Ryan threw his hands up in defense. "Before you blow a gasket, hear me out."

"Too late on the gasket, you fucker!" Anderson bellowed.

"Shhh," Ryan hissed. "Do you want her to hear you?"

"No!" Anderson barked quietly. "No, this is between you and me."

Ryan narrowed his eyes at that, wondering at the enigmatic comment. Surely Anderson didn't have feelings for Ginny. Did he?

"Are you going to listen? Let me explain?"

Anderson waved his hand in a "proceed" gesture and Ryan started. "Things didn't turn out the way I expected Friday night at the club."

"Of course they didn't," Anderson interjected. "I knew you'd bitten off more than you could chew taking her there alone."

Ryan ignored his friend's comment. "Liam the asswipe was there performing mouth-to-mouth on some busty blonde. Ginny was hurt and I made a few unwise comments—"

"Shocking," Anderson added.

"If you keep insulting me, I'm gonna get pissed off too and we can't really afford to refurnish this office after I kick your ass. Besides, I already broke the phone."

"You know, I'm not so sure it'd be my ass getting kicked, but please go on. I'd love to hear all about how you seduced our best friend after she'd been jilted by her boyfriend. No doubt she was feeling vulnerable and you were right there ready to swoop in, take advantage of her."

Ryan shook his head in disbelief. "When in our entire lives have you ever seen Ginny vulnerable? That girl is tough as nails and mean as a snake when crossed."

"When did you start calling her Ginny?"

Ryan felt all the anger seep out of his body. "I'm in love with her, Charlie."

He expected to see shock, confusion, any number of emotions on his friend's face—but he certainly didn't expect to see Charlie smile.

"I was starting to think you'd never come around."

"What's that supposed to mean?" Ryan asked.

"You've been in love with Ginny Brooks since we were twelve."

"Bullshit."

Anderson laughed. "'Fraid not, my friend. It seemed pretty obvious to everyone, except you and Brooks that is. You forget, I was there for that first kiss."

Ryan fell into one of the office chairs and considered Anderson's words. Was it possible?

"Damn fool," Anderson added, taking the seat next to him. "Think about it, Travers. Every time that girl brought a new boyfriend around, you went out of your way to make the guy look like a loser. All those names you called them."

"She dated a lot of jerks."

"No she didn't." Anderson placed a hand on his shoulder. "Couple of those guys were pretty nice. Would have made her good husbands if it weren't for you pointing out all of their flaws, making Brooks doubt the relationships."

"You're making me sound like a prick," Ryan said, wondering if it was his fault Ginny wasn't happily married with a family of her own.

"Not a prick, just an idiot in love."

"I wouldn't make a good husband. I can't marry Brooks," Ryan said, suddenly seeing his treatment of Ginny over the past years clearly. He had discouraged her romances, scared off her boyfriends. He'd made damn sure she was alone, all because he couldn't stand the thought of another man having what he wanted.

"Jesus, Anderson. I've screwed up everything."

"What do you mean you wouldn't be a good husband? You're nuts about the girl. No man would ever love her more than you."

"I'm too controlling, demanding…too impulsive. I'm completely unreliable—hell, I'm always late!"

"Do you honestly think in twenty years Brooks hasn't seen all of that? She knows what she's getting with you and given what I just saw in that office a few minutes ago, she doesn't seem to mind."

"But sexually—" Ryan began.

"Did you take her back to your room at the club?" Anderson asked. His friend was well aware of his sexual practices—it was one of the things the two men had in common.

"Yes."

"Did she run from the room screaming?"

Ryan grinned as he recalled exactly what kind of screaming Ginny did in that room. "She was a bit too tied up to do any running."

"Shit," Anderson said, looking at his face. "Don't say another word. I don't want to know. I love that girl like a sister and I think if you try to tell me any details, I'll have to kill you."

"Let's just say she wasn't scared."

"Well, I could've told you that. Ginny's never scared. She's perfect for you…in every way, so accept it and move on. There's no way I'm going to let you waste another twenty years of her life while you're trying to screw your head on right. Go marry her. Make babies. Be happy."

Ryan closed his eyes, the image of Ginny with his baby at her breast winding its way around his hopes and dreams for the future until marriage and a family was all he wanted.

"You're right."

The door banged open and Taylor stormed in. "Where's the fire?"

Ryan looked at Anderson, who suddenly looked guilty. "I called him before I woke you up."

"What's the matter, Anderson? Didn't think you could take me alone?" Ryan teased.

"Why are we beating you up?" Taylor asked, not looking too concerned about the prospect of kicking some ass. It appeared Anderson's call had woken him up and he wouldn't mind hitting someone.

"He found me in a compromising position with Ginny," Ryan answered.

"Who's Ginny?" Taylor asked, and Anderson and Ryan burst into laughter.

"Brooks," Anderson replied.

"I'm going to fucking kill you," Taylor said, his fists clenched as he approached Ryan.

"No you're not," Ryan assured him, still laughing.

"Why not?"

"Because I love her and I'm going to marry her."

* * *

Ginny heard murmured voices in the outer offices and blushed to realize she was lying on the couch in Ryan's office, naked, except for the shirt he had obviously covered her with. Rising, she crossed the room to retrieve her clothing. She slid on the skirt and her shoes, but decided her blouse was a lost cause. She threw Ryan's shirt on, buttoning it and rolling up the sleeves until they no longer swallowed her hands. She tried to move quickly in case the voices she heard decided to come into his office. She could hear Ryan's deep, dulcet tones, and as she listened she realized the other voice belonged to Anderson.

Tiptoeing to the door, she opened it a crack, wondering if Anderson had seen them together and trying to decide how she'd face him if he had.

Ryan was speaking. "I wouldn't make a good husband. I can't marry Brooks. Jesus, Anderson. I've screwed up everything."

Ginny quietly closed the door, the loud crash of her heart shattering drowning out Anderson's response.

Ryan regretted it. All of it.

She struggled to suck in a breath and fought back the nausea that was attacking her in waves. Air. She needed fresh air. Rushing to the window, she threw it open, thrusting her head out into the cool night breeze. All she could think about was escape. She had to escape. Get away from here.

No. Dammit, no! She'd run from Ryan once and she wouldn't do that again. She was in love with him, and she'd had more than enough of the foolish man's games. If this was only sex to him, he was in for a rude awakening because she wouldn't settle for that. She wanted him, his body, his heart, his mind. She wanted his friendship and his love. Hell, after spending the last twenty years making excuses for his tardiness, organizing his desk and business affairs, listening to his locker-room talk, he owed her.

She loved him. God help her, but she really, truly loved him.

I wouldn't make a good husband. Husband? Travers? Was he considering marriage? Shit, she was still trying to get used to the idea that she loved the man, and he'd already made—and dismissed—the leap to 'til death do us part.

Although…why was marriage out of the question? She loved him and, after thinking about Allie's comments all weekend, she was beginning to suspect Ryan loved her as well. He'd hated every man she'd ever dated on sight. He was so furious the night she'd lost her virginity she'd thought he would punch a hole in the wall. At the time, she'd thought it was because he'd disliked Erik, but he'd made a comment Friday night that kept floating back to her. I've had a hankering to have you at my mercy ever since you were eighteen and gave your virginity to that dipshit Erik.

Was he upset that she'd slept with someone other than him? Had he wanted to be her first?

God, he'd already claimed that title in so many other respects.

The more she thought about it, the more she was convinced they were perfect for each other, and if he couldn't see that, she would just have to prove it to him.

But how?

A thought came to her. A plan so deliciously devious it might just work. Rushing to the desk, Ginny reached down and scooped up Ryan's cell phone before returning to the window. Swinging her leg over the windowsill, she jumped down to the ground—grateful for their single-story office building—and started dialing Allie's number. She was going to need help.

Chapter Nine

"Crap. I knew it was a mistake to let you in Saturday morning."

"Oh hush, Allie. You're loving every minute of this and you know it. You've done nothing but talk about coming to this club since the place opened."

"Ginny Brooks. When I said I wanted to come to the Way Down Under Club, believe me when I say this was not what I had in mind." Allie grabbed the jumbo bag of M&M's out of the grocery sack and sighed. "God, I'm probably going to need therapy after this."

Ginny giggled nervously. Usually she was grateful for her sister's sense of humor, but tonight it wasn't helping to ease the so-called butterflies that were attacking her stomach like a swarm of locusts. After she'd escaped Ryan's office on Monday night, she had called her sister and asked her to pick her up at the end of the block. Together, they'd hit an all-night convenience store and cleaned out the candy aisle.

"You better hope all this candy sweetens him up," Allie said.

They'd been loading their sugary booty into Allie's car when Ryan's cell phone rang. To say he was pissed off that she'd run again—this time with his phone—was probably an understatement.

Allie was still chatting away, oblivious to Ginny's anxiety. "Anderson said he hit the roof Monday night when you told him you weren't coming into work this week and that you'd be out of reach for a few days."

"Yeah, well. It's for his own good. Mom always said, 'Absence makes the heart grow fonder'. Maybe if he weren't so stubbornly attached to his bachelor status, I wouldn't have had to go through all of this."

Allie shook her head. "Anderson said he and Taylor have been taking all their meetings out of the office this week just to avoid running into Travers. They said he's like a volcano about to erupt."

"Dammit, Allie! Shut up about what Anderson is saying. I know what I'm doing." She didn't mean to snap at her sister, but she was terrified and not at all certain she wasn't making a gigantic mistake.

Allie fell silent and continued unloading the candy.

"I'm sorry," Ginny said softly. "I'm a nervous wreck, but that doesn't give me the right to take it out on you."

Allie grinned and Ginny knew she'd been forgiven as easily as that. It was one of the best things about her sister. None of their fights—and they'd had millions in their lifetime—ever lasted beyond the apology. "You're going to knock his socks off, sis. You are so hot, you're going to melt the chocolate."

Ginny's hands instinctively reached up to her hair. After their midnight candy run, she and Allie had driven into the city, checked into a swanky hotel and treated themselves to a day at a spa. She'd let her sister talk her into a new hairstyle to go along with the highlights. She'd kept most of the length, opting for more layers, simply because she suspected Ryan liked her hair long.

"What time is it?" Ginny asked nervously.

"Time to get you ready. Anderson and Taylor should be here with Travers in a few minutes. I'll just get you situated and then mark the trail."

Ginny nodded. They'd called Anderson a couple of days earlier to recruit his help. Once they'd told him their plan, he'd jumped on board and dragged Taylor along with him for the ride.

"So get undressed and lay down," Allie prompted.

Ginny blushed despite the fact she and Allie had shared a room the whole time they were growing up.

Tonight, however, was definitely pushing the boundaries of sisterly love.

"Hurry your ass up or I'm not going to have time to work my magic." Or perhaps they weren't pushing anything at all. Ginny shook her head and marveled again at Allie's complete lack of the embarrassment gene. Nothing fazed her sister…ever.

She stripped off her clothes and positioned herself spread-eagle on the bed. She and Allie giggled as Allie set the stage for the night. Ginny couldn't wait to see Ryan's face when he saw her.

Please, she silently prayed, please let this work.

* * *

"Listen, I appreciate you guys trying to cheer me up, but I told you, I'm not depressed. I'm pissed. I'm going to find Miss Ginny Brooks and beat her ass for this disappearing act. I really need to be home in case she calls."

"Face it, buddy," Taylor said, slapping him on the shoulder. "She hasn't called all week and she's not going to call tonight. She said she'd find you when the time was right. Come on, it's Friday night. Let's live it up a little."

Ryan picked up his beer and took a long swig. He'd been going out of his mind for days wondering where Ginny had gone, why she'd run away from him again. Damn woman was driving him insane. When he'd called her Monday night after finding her and his phone missing, she'd merely said she was taking a little trip. She'd said she needed to do some thinking and that she'd be back. Then she'd warned him not to look for her and not to worry.

Yeah right. Like that was possible. He'd torn the town apart twice looking for her before finally admitting that she'd flown the coop and covered her tracks well.

"What the hell is she doing here?"

Ryan looked up, surprised by the annoyed tone in Anderson's voice. He watched, amazed, as Allie Brooks sauntered into the bar like she owned the place. Several men approached her, and she smiled and flirted with all of them before moving forward. Ryan glanced over and noticed that Anderson's face appeared to be carved in granite and his fists were white from clenching the table so tightly.

She walked straight up to where they sat and smiled at him. "Hey, Travers."

"Where the fuck is Ginny?" He suspected Ginny's sister, who'd been missing this week as well, knew exactly where his wayward girlfriend was.

"Oh, you know, she's around. She would have joined us for a drink, but she's kind of tied up at the moment."

Ryan stood and gripped Allie's elbow. The girl had been a pain in the ass since grade school, always trailing around after their group, teasing them, causing trouble. "Listen, Allie, I'm not in the mood for your games."

A firm hand on his wrist distracted him. "Take your hand off her, Travers."

Ryan looked over at the undeniable fury in Anderson's face and he released Allie's arm.

Allie giggled and patted Ryan's cheek affectionately. "Ginny wanted me to give you this."

Ryan grabbed the envelope from her hand and stepped away from the table. Ripping it open, he found a message written in Ginny's handwriting.

Sugar and Spice and everything nice lies at the end of the rainbow.

What the fuck did that mean?

Allie walked over to him and handed him an empty bag of M&Ms. "The hallway," she whispered.

Rapidly walking out of the bar, Ryan was instantly greeted by a line of colorful chocolate candies, leading down the hallway through the club. Following the line, he found himself standing outside the door to his own room. His heart was racing. What was Ginny's game?

He opened the door and stepped inside. The room was dimly lit, the light of a few candles providing the only illumination. He noticed the trail of candy continued at his feet and led straight to the bed. His eyes followed the line—and he found her.

He blinked several times, trying to understand and believe the tableau before him.

Ginny was naked and bound on the bed. As he approached, he could see her wrists and ankles were tied spread-eagle with cherry licorice laces. She wore a candy necklace around her neck and on each nipple rested a Hershey's kiss. Her pussy—good God, her shaved, bare pussy—was artfully decorated with whipped cream and someone had created an intricate pattern on her chest with SweeTARTS. The pattern mimicked the one he'd created with the hemp rope just a week ago.

He looked at her face and then narrowed his eyes. "What the hell did you do to your hair?"

Ginny giggled at his question, and he was aware it was the same one he'd asked last Friday.

"I got it cut. Do you like it?"

"Shit, it looks hot as hell. Ginny?" he asked. He was so shocked by her appearance that he forgot his anger in an instant.

"I love you," she said before he could formulate his next question.

He frowned, confused. She loved him. She'd run away from him and hidden—twice. Now she was lying in his bed like some candy man's wet dream telling him she loved him.

"I don't—"

She cut him off. "I heard you talking to Anderson Monday night. I heard what you said about us being a mistake and I—"

"I never said that," he retorted quickly. What the hell was she talking about?

"You said you'd screwed up. That you couldn't marry me. I wanted to prove that you're wrong."

She'd heard only a small part of his conversation with Anderson and had obviously taken everything he'd said completely out of context. Ryan was relieved and furious at the same time. Once again, she'd run off before he could explain.

Or had she? What was she doing in this bed?

"I'm wrong?" he asked.

"We're perfect together, Travers. Absolutely, positively perfect in every way and I don't care how long it takes or what I have to do, I will prove that to you."

"And this," Ryan pointed to the candy adorning her body, "is your proof?"

She offered him one of her breathtaking smiles, and he felt his heart expand at the sight of it.

"Everyone knows you have a sweet tooth, but I know you also like things a bit spicy, so I thought I'd give you both."

Ryan laughed. "God, I love you."

Her eyes widened. "You do?"

"Yes. If you'd stuck around to eavesdrop on the rest of my conversation with Anderson, you would have heard me say so. Ginny, I love you. I. Love. You. Dammit, you're an impulsive, headstrong, demanding little thing. And I'm crazy about you."

She grinned at his name-calling. “Oh yeah? Well, you never take anything serious, you’re too controlling and you’re always late.”

“Like you said, we’re the perfect couple,” he joked before swiftly placing a kiss on her lips.

“Ryan—”

“Marry me, Ginny Brooks. I’m getting too old to keep chasing your boyfriends off.”

“Is that what you’ve been doing?”

“Isn’t it? Say you’ll marry me. Say the words.”

“Isn’t it supposed to be a marriage proposal, not a marriage demand?”

“Ginny…” he answered, his voice gruff and commanding.

“Fine. I’ll marry you. I mean, let’s face it, it’s not like anybody else could put up with—”

Ryan captured her lips with his, silencing her words. When he felt her fall into the kiss, he pulled away, his mouth lightly touching her own as he spoke. “I love you, Ginny Brooks. You’re my sugar and spice all rolled into one delicious package. Now—can I have some candy?”

Everything Nice

What Women Want, book 2

Charlie's wants Allie. Allie and Alex want each other—and Charlie. But does Charlie want Alex? Plunging headfirst into a ménage is one way to find out…

After Alex confesses to Allie that he wants both her and his best friend, Charlie, in his bed, Allie skips town like a thief in the night. Now, six years later, Allie is back in their lives, all grown up and more alluring than ever. What starts as a night of three friends catching up turns into intimate explorations in Charlie's truck…and Alex's shower…and his king-size bed…

While Alex and Allie are thrilled with the threesome, Charlie struggles with the idea of sharing Allie, and with his newfound feelings for his best friend. A hot encounter at the office—with Alex bent over his desk—only confuses Charlie further. It's up to Alex and Allie to convince him that two plus one can equal love.

Everything Nice, a sequel to Sugar and Spice, offers intense scenes of male-on-male sex and heart-stopping ménage

Dedication

This story is dedicated to my parents, who are very proud of their daughter, the writer, even though they've been forbidden from reading any of her books.

By the way, you can't read this one either, Mom and Dad! I love you.

Prologue

Allie Brooks leaned back against a log, gazing into the bonfire and enjoying the pleasant buzz of the alcohol flowing through her body. Travers, Taylor and Anderson were throwing an end-of-summer bash out by the river to celebrate the first anniversary of their successful engineering firm, and Allie was having a great time, although she was fairly sure she'd be sorry about the number of beers she'd consumed tomorrow. She glanced down at the pile of empty bottles by her feet and tried to remember if they were all hers.

While she was happy for the group of men and her sister—who was serving as their office manager—she couldn't help but feel a bit envious. She'd been hanging around since her high school graduation four years earlier, waiting for her life to begin, while her sister Ginny seemed to have her future all mapped out. Allie was still living at home and working at a job she hated, despite the fact her mother's cancer had gone into remission ages ago.

Just last night, she'd been offered a new job, a better job. Shit, the world's greatest job. Yet instead of being thrilled, she sat alone, watching the flames and contemplating the idea of moving away from the only home she'd ever known to take a chance at fulfilling her dream of seeing the world. She should be screaming her excitement from the rooftops, but something seemed to be holding her back.

Glancing across the bonfire, she watched Charlie Anderson talking to Travers. Anderson looked especially hot tonight in his cut-off jean shorts and dark green T-shirt. She admired how the T-shirt was just tight enough to accentuate his perfect pecs. He was wearing his light brown hair longer these days, and she admired the tousled look as he ran his fingers through it, pushing it off his face. At some point, she supposed she would have to get over her schoolgirl infatuation with her sister's friend, but—like everything else in her life—that plan seemed to be on hold too.

She'd been sitting here for nearly an hour studying the man's perfection in relative anonymity. "Relative" being the operative term, as Alex Taylor came and planted himself beside her on the ground, and she realized she hadn't been as careful as she should have.

"So how long have you been in love with Anderson?" Taylor asked.

Allie turned to look at him briefly before letting her gaze drift back to the man in question. “Forever,” she confessed, the alcohol loosening her tongue. “How long have you been in love with him?”

Her question was nothing more than a taunt, a petty way to strike out against the man, and she expected him to ignore her challenge, offer a flat-out denial, call her a fool.

She’d only come to suspect Taylor’s feelings toward his best friend since they’d moved home from college. For some reason, after their return, she’d begun to watch Taylor as much as Anderson. A fact she couldn’t even begin to explain to herself as the man had been a thorn in her side for most of their childhood. To say they butted heads often was an understatement. Ginny had teased her about her volatile relationship with Taylor, once claiming that they were both too much alike.

She was surprised to hear his heavy sigh of resignation.

“How did you know?” he asked.

Allie offered him a light laugh despite the fact her heart felt far from happy. “I’m not blind.”

Taylor nodded as if her answer were enough. “It would seem that blindness only affects Anderson.”

“He doesn’t know?”

Taylor chuckled, though the sound offered no mirth. “Never came up in conversation.”

"In twelve years?"

"He's not gay, Allie."

She raised her eyebrows at his words. "I wouldn't have said you were either, if your list of female conquests was any indication."

"You're right. I'm not gay," he admitted. He turned away from watching Anderson and moved closer to her. His intent gaze, while making her uneasy, drew her toward him like a moth to a flame.

"Care to explain that statement?" she asked, the alcohol in her system making her say things she'd never have had the nerve to voice otherwise.

"Ever heard the term bisexual?" he replied sarcastically.

She scowled, but before she could chastise him for being such a smartass, he grinned at her and ran his hand down her cheek in a more-than-friendly way. "Allie, I love women too. I love being with women, making love to them, tasting and touching them."

"But you've been with men as well?"

"A couple in college," he confessed.

"Neither of them stole your heart?" she asked, silently wondering why it felt so natural to be having this far-from-normal conversation with a man she'd always suspected detested her.

"My heart's not available," he answered simply.

"It belongs to Anderson?"

Taylor glanced back at his friend. "He's the only man I've ever truly found myself attracted to—in a forever kind of way. I can't help wondering what it would be like to be with him."

She nodded. "Well, that certainly explains why you hate me. I never realized it before, but I suppose I'm the competition."

Taylor's eyebrows lowered, furrowed. "I don't hate you, Allie. I never have."

Allie was surprised by his answer. "But I thought—"

"Allie," Taylor interrupted, moving closer to her. "You aren't the competition. You're part of the equation."

Before she could respond, his lips lowered to hers, taking them in a kiss that was gentle and hard at the same time, tentative and possessive in the same breath.

She tried to understand what was happening, but the alcohol left her brain feeling fuzzy, while Taylor's kisses and roving hands left her body feeling very warm.

When he pulled back, Allie opened her eyes. "I'm drunk. And confused," she admitted, and Taylor laughed, drawing his finger softly down her cheek again.

"Soon, hellion. Soon it'll all work out. You'll see." And with that enigmatic comment, Taylor got up and walked around the bonfire, joining in the conversation with Travers and Anderson.

Allie took a deep breath and struggled to understand what just happened. She looked around at the other people at the party. No one seemed to have noticed Taylor kissing her, everyone engrossed in their own conversations.

What the hell am I doing?

Kissing Alex Taylor—a confessed bisexual who happened to be in love with the same man as she—was not smart.

Shit, she was drunk and depressed about her life. Her mind was playing tricks on her. There was no way she could have possibly understood Taylor's intentions correctly. He couldn't have meant that he intended to have her and Anderson, could he?

She struggled to take a deep breath, and a feeling of claustrophobia closed in on her as she realized she could give in to his desires far too easily. Apparently Ginny had been right. She and Taylor were similar people with similar hopes and needs.

But if she succumbed to Taylor's invitation, where would that leave her?

Here, she thought sadly. Stuck in this same godforsaken town, waiting tables at the fucking diner. The image of her exciting new job offer floated before her eyes.

Stay or leave?

Stay or leave?

She felt someone watching her, and her gaze traveled to Anderson. She saw him studying her, his eyebrows lowered. So many emotions seemed to be controlling his face, she couldn't tell what he was thinking or feeling. Curiosity, anger, jealousy, concern?

So she'd been wrong. One person had seen the kiss. One person had seen it all.

Chapter One

Six years later

"Well, now that you've finished your part in this little scheme of your sister's, what do you say I drive you home?" Charlie offered his arm to Allie, anxious to get her out of the Way Down Under Club. It was a sex club, and God only knew what kind of mischief she would get into if he didn't get her out of here.

He'd only agreed to let her come in the first place because her sister Ginny had set her sights on his partner and friend, Ryan Travers. After nearly twenty years of friendship, the pair had fallen head over heels in love and Charlie couldn't be happier for them. Earlier in the evening, Ginny and Allie had set up a bit of a love trap for his unsuspecting friend.

He, Travers and Taylor were part owners of the club, and Charlie knew the fact that she was with them would offer some protection from the men who might approach her—particularly the Doms.

"Are you nuts?" Allie protested. "I've been waiting for months to see inside this place. There is no way I'm going home now. Besides, it's still early."

"I think 'months' is pushing it a bit, considering you've only been back in town a few weeks. And you are most definitely going home." Charlie had known this would happen. He glanced over at Taylor, expecting support, and was surprised to see his best friend merely shrug.

"I don't see any harm in her staying. Why don't we all have a drink and afterward, Anderson and I can give you a tour of the place?" Taylor suggested, and his nonchalant words floored Charlie.

"Are you nuts?" Charlie asked, repeating Allie's phrase. "We're not giving her a tour of this place!"

"Oh stuff it, Anderson. I'm twenty-eight years old and I don't need you trying to protect my innocence anymore. I lost that a long time ago."

Her words were light and accompanied by a playful giggle, but Charlie felt them like a blow to his gut.

"Allie," he started.

She reached up and cupped his face gently. Her smile was genuine and sweet. "You were wonderful to me when I was younger. Sweeter than any true big brother could have been. You could have brushed me aside as Ginny's tagalong, annoying kid sister, but you never did and I appreciate that, really. But I stopped needing your protection a long time ago. I've grown up."

Taylor laughed, shaking his head. He directed Allie to a chair at the corner table where they'd been sitting earlier. "I don't think you need to worry about Charlie viewing you in a respectable, brotherly way."

Charlie scowled at his friend's joke, but Taylor ignored him. "What would you like to drink, Allie?"

She took the seat Taylor proffered. "A glass of white wine, please."

Taylor gestured for the waiter then sat down to her left. Charlie felt like an ass standing alone so he resumed his own seat.

"I have to admit I'm a bit annoyed with you, Allie Brooks," Taylor said.

"Me?"

"You've been back in town nearly a month and you've yet to spend any quality time with us."

Allie smiled. "I've been too busy playing Cupid with Ginny and trying to get settled in at my new place. I swear I've scoured this whole damn town looking for a decent home to buy, but I've determined there isn't one. I may have to ask you boys to build me a house."

"So you're just renting the townhouse?" Taylor asked.

"Yes," Allie nodded. "I have a definite idea of where I want to settle down, but it's difficult to find the right piece of land. I'd like to build a house on the lake like you guys did."

"The lake is a great place to live," Taylor answered.

Charlie tried to bite back the frustration over being left out of their casual conversation. He glanced around the room and counted at least three men eyeing Allie with definite interest. He gave each of them a proprietary look meant to leave no doubt that she was unavailable, and the men turned away.

"Are you ready to go yet?" he asked, interrupting their stimulating conversation about property values.

"I haven't even gotten my wine," Allie argued.

"Don't mind Anderson," Taylor said to her. "He lost his sense of humor several years ago. Six, to be exact."

Charlie clenched his fists under the table and considered clobbering his best friend for his unexpected, revealing comment.

"Six years ago?" Allie asked, and Charlie thought she'd gone a bit pale. He was going to kill Taylor when they got home.

"He's kidding," Charlie added quickly, though even to his own ears the words sounded like a lie.

He'd been worried sick when Allie had taken off six years earlier. Ginny had tried to explain Allie's hasty departure, but he'd never really forgiven her for leaving without saying goodbye. While they'd never crossed the boundary from friendship to relationship, somewhere in the back of his mind he'd always nurtured the belief that she belonged to him. Throughout his entire life, he'd believed that she was his to care for.

When she'd skipped town like a thief in the night, he'd felt as if a large part of his soul had simply vanished. He was fairly certain he would have lost his mind if not for Taylor's steadfast friendship.

"I should have said goodbye…explained why I was leaving." Allie placed her hand on Charlie's knee. "I just thought…"

"Thought what?" Charlie asked.

"That you would try to stop me."

"I would have." He replied so quickly he realized it was true. He would never have let her run off with Jim Griffin, regardless of the innocuous job description.

"Charlie," she said softly, and he struggled to catch his breath at the sound of his name on her lips. "I'm sorry I didn't say goodbye, but I don't regret one single second of my time away. I'll never apologize for that."

Taylor leaned forward and chuckled softly, no doubt hoping to lighten the suddenly tense mood at the table. "No one's asking for apologies or explanations tonight. We're just three friends, catching up on the good old days."

Charlie appreciated his friend's maneuver as it gave him precious time to gather his wits about him. Sometimes he was amazed how in tune to his emotions his best friend seemed to be.

"Ah good. Our drinks." Taylor took the glass of wine the waiter delivered and set it in front of Allie. "You know, hellion, I think these last few weeks are the longest you've stayed in one place in years. Aren't you getting bored hanging around this lazy town yet? Doesn't seem to me like there'd be enough excitement around here to keep you occupied."

Charlie heard the challenge in Taylor's tone and realized his friend's thoughts mirrored his own. He'd long ago resigned himself to the fact that Allie had an adventurous streak a mile wide. Ginny had kept them abreast of Allie's escapades during the past few years.

She'd taken off with barely a word to anyone with Jim Griffin, and Charlie still couldn't think of the man without a growl rising in his chest. For one thing, Griffin had been roommates with Allie's father in college. The damn man had also been rich enough to do whatever the hell he pleased, which unfortunately meant risking his life—and Allie's—on a daily basis.

Charlie fought back a scowl as he recalled listening to Ginny describe Allie's adventures with Griffin. They'd bungee jumped off the Zambezi Bridge in Victoria Falls, skydived in Moab, Arizona, snorkeled in shark-infested waters and even driven a race car at

Talladega. If there was an element of danger involved in an activity, Griffin was the first person in line to try it, usually with Allie at his heels.

She'd traveled around the world with him, serving as his traveling companion and personal assistant, and Charlie couldn't help but wonder just how personally she'd served the man. Damn woman was a free spirit with far too much independence and stubbornness for his peace of mind.

"Oh I think the last few years with Jim managed to burn out any aspirations I might have had in terms of living my life as a drifter. Believe me, if I never see the inside of another hotel room again, it'll be too soon," she joked lightly before the usual sadness that always crept in when she mentioned Griffin fell into place. "I do miss that crazy man."

Griffin had died six months earlier of a massive heart attack and, while it appeared that she was at last ready to put down some roots, Charlie wondered what her return would mean for him. His feelings for the woman were such a jumble in his head and heart, he didn't know which way was up. When her sister had mentioned Allie was returning home, he'd decided that hell would freeze over before he'd let her escape him again.

Unfortunately his work commitments and Allie's busy schedule—moving back home and settling Griffin's vast estate—had interfered with any plans he might have had in terms of taking the next step. Seeing her tonight, looking so beautiful, had solidified his determination to cast off their "just friends" relationship and attempt to build something more.

"So what's the plan, Allie? Got your future all figured out yet?" Taylor asked before Charlie could formulate the question. He glanced up at his friend and wondered for the millionth time if Taylor could actually read his mind.

"I guess I decided it was time to settle down and…" She paused, shrugging lightly.

"Stop running." Taylor finished her comment, and Charlie wondered what his friend thought Allie was running from. Him? The thought made his blood run cold.

"I wasn't running," she replied hotly.

"You could have fooled me," Taylor answered with a cocky grin.

"Am I missing something here?" Charlie asked.

Allie grinned at him and shook her head. "Nope, Taylor is just being his typical know-it-all self. Apparently he thinks every decision I make in my life is directly influenced by him."

Taylor laughed at her insult. She and Taylor had returned to their "put-downs as means of communication" the day Allie returned home, although Charlie noticed these new insults had taken on a decidedly racy tone. “Face it, hellion, you just couldn’t stay away from my hot body any longer.”

Allie rolled her eyes. “Thank God I had a light dinner. I feel fairly certain that inane comment would have brought it right back up.”

As seemed to be the case any time he was alone with them, Charlie felt his patience slipping away at the thought that he was an outsider to some secret these two shared.

They damn well better not have any secrets, he thought.

“Allie, get your purse. I’m taking you home. This is no place for you,” he announced when yet another man looked as if he wanted to approach her. The Doms were circling like fucking sharks, and he had no intention of letting them sink their teeth into this prey.

Allie turned to look at him and once again he was blown away by how beautiful she looked tonight. She’d always been pretty, but there was a maturity in her lovely face that hadn’t been there when she’d left. She’d shed her young woman cuteness and drifted into grown woman knockout. Her long, dark hair was naturally wavy and her deep green eyes were alluring, stunning. Charlie was used to her appearance drawing the gaze of every man in her vicinity. It had certainly captured and held his attention for years.

She shook her head. “I don’t want to leave yet. I want to stay here. With you…and Taylor.” Her voice was husky, sexy, and the look she gave him left no doubt in his mind that the fact they were in a sex club wasn't lost on her.

He fought the ingrained instinct that screamed at him to grab her hand and pull her to the nearest bedroom. He wanted her with a desire that bordered on primal, but he found himself fighting his attraction tonight because—despite their constant jibing—he suspected that Taylor was interested in her as well. He and his best friend had never fought over a woman and Charlie didn't want to now.

Nevertheless, he was fairly certain a war for Allie's affections was looming on the horizon, and he knew there was no way in hell he could walk away from her, even if Taylor was attracted to her.

Taylor leaned closer to Allie, and Charlie struggled to take a breath. Allie's chair was backed into a corner with the two of them flanking her, partially hiding her from the room as a whole. The table was covered with a long cloth that Charlie noticed was shielding Taylor's roving hand from the view of every occupant in the bar, except for him.

"Taylor," he muttered quickly, intending his word to be a protest, a warning, but well aware his tone fell short of that mark.

Taylor grinned at him as his hand drifted over Allie's skirt, and he gave him a look that couldn't be misconstrued as anything less than a dare. What did his friend expect? That he'd cuss him out? Start a fight? Walk away?

Charlie glanced down and Taylor gripped Allie's bare knee with his right hand, while his eyes never left Charlie's face. The short skirt she was wearing only covered her to mid-thigh. As Taylor's hand crept up her leg, Charlie looked up at her face, expecting to see and hear her refusal at being touched so intimately in a public place.

He was shocked by the look of desire in her eyes. She wanted Taylor to touch her. Charlie was blown away by the realization and again he felt like an outsider, but he couldn't move from the table, couldn't leave them alone, even if it was the proper, polite thing to do.

"Get your hand off her, Taylor." His voice was quiet, but only a fool wouldn't hear the anger.

Taylor's fingers traveled along the hem of her skirt before disappearing beneath the lacy garment.

"It doesn't have to be either-or," Taylor whispered, still looking at him.

Charlie watched as a lovely flush colored her porcelain cheeks and he heard her soft intake of breath.

"Allie," Charlie said, determined to save her if that's what she wanted. One look at her proved she wasn't opposed to Taylor's touch.

"You're so soft and warm," Taylor murmured, turning to look at her with a gentle smile. Then, to

Charlie's shock, his friend spoke to him. "Touch her, Charlie."

Charlie shook his head as too many things came crashing down on him at once. For one, he and Taylor hadn't used each other's first names since the sixth grade. Secondly, it sounded as if his best friend was suggesting they both stick their hands up Allie Brooks' skirt.

Charlie looked back at Allie. Her breathing was labored, and Charlie could tell Taylor was definitely hitting the right buttons below her waist. Just how far had his hand traveled?

"Do it," Taylor repeated and, as he spoke, Allie's gaze traveled to him. Rather than panic or fear, she offered him a sweet, inviting smile.

"Please," she whispered.

"God dammit, Allie," Charlie muttered, but before he could say more, she interrupted him.

"I want you to touch me, Charlie. I want you and Alex to touch me," she stated simply.

He tried to understand where the hell he'd lost control of this evening's events, but his confusion was overpowered by his own needs and desires. He'd wanted Allie for too long and with too much passion to continue to deny it. His left hand wandered to her thigh as if on autopilot. Her legs parted at his stroke and he slowly caressed the soft skin on her inner leg, his fingers itching to find the heat that had kept him awake too many nights these past few years. The heat that had him jerking off in the dark, her name on his lips.

When he grazed her panties—hallelujah, a thong—he discovered that Taylor had already pulled aside the thin strap and had one finger buried in her pussy.

"You're perfect," Alex whispered to Allie, whose eyes were glazed with longing.

"Oh God," she breathed. "Touch me, Charlie. Please."

Charlie felt the bonds of his worry fall away at her words. He dragged his finger over her clit, relishing her soft whimpers, but he knew in an instant that one small bit of contact wasn't enough. He had to be inside her. He needed to touch, to feel, to appreciate the wet, glorious heat Taylor was experiencing.

His friend looked up at him, compassion in his gaze. They were in this together. Charlie could see it in Alex's face, the two of them able to communicate without words. An understanding born from years of friendship.

God, when had he started to think of his friend as "Alex" rather than "Taylor"?

Charlie reached down to her opening and drove a single finger inside her, alongside Alex's. Their knuckles rubbed together as they slowly moved in and out of her in unison.

The moment should have felt strange, wrong—anything other than this perfect melding of three.

Allie's inner muscles clenched against their gently moving fingers, announcing her imminent climax. Her response reminded Charlie that they were in a very public setting. Despite the fact they were in a sex club, the bar area was typically off-limits for what they were doing. There were other rooms where this behavior was permissible.

He felt Alex's hand retreat, and he heard Allie's outraged hiss at his departure.

A strong, reassuring hand landed on his shoulder. "Charlie."

He looked up, surprised to see Alex had risen. As always, he felt as though his thoughts, his concerns had been laid bare before his friend, and he saw empathy in Alex's gaze.

"You were right," his friend said. "We should take her home."

"What?" Allie cried out indignantly, but Charlie heard the inflection in his friend's words, and he slowly pulled his finger out of her heavenly body. He knew they wouldn't be taking Allie to her home but to theirs.

They'd bought property on the lake several years ago once the engineering firm was established and making money, and they'd built a large duplex. Somehow the idea made sense as they'd been roommates since college, sharing first a dorm and then an apartment.

The idea that they would take Allie there together left him uncertain, uneasy. This wasn't his plan. Fuck, he'd never in his wildest dreams imagined sharing this woman, any woman, with his best friend. Where the hell was Alex leading them? Where would this leave his plans for a future with Allie?

"It's time," Alex said. "Hell, I'd say it's past time."

The conviction in Alex's voice and in his face had Charlie rising from the table, grinning. Charlie would never have considered sharing a woman with anyone but Alex. Now that he thought about it, he wouldn't consider it with any woman but Allie.

"Alex," he said, feeling as though they should say more to each other. This certainly wasn't the kind of decision one made based on impulse.

"Trust me." Alex's quietly spoken request resonated inside him as Charlie considered his words. He trusted Alex implicitly, maybe more than he'd ever trusted anyone in his life.

"Okay," he said, looking down at Allie.

"Are you two trying to kill me?" Allie asked breathlessly. "You can't get me that close to coming and then drop me at my house!"

Alex grabbed one of her hands while Charlie reached for the other.

"I don't recall saying anything about taking you to your house," Alex said as they pulled her up.

"But I—"

"Come home with us," Charlie whispered in her ear. The idea of what Alex was proposing—what they were both proposing to her—appealed to him more than he could say, despite the slight feeling of unease nipping at his conscience.

"It's time to stop running," Alex added, and Allie's eyes widened at his repeated taunt.

Is this what Allie had left town to escape? Had Alex made this same proposal to her that night by the bonfire? Charlie's heart raced as he recalled the kiss he'd witnessed. The thought that his friend had perhaps wanted this for so many years staggered him.

"Okay," she answered simply, and Charlie struggled to suck in a deep breath at her assent. She wanted to be with them. Both of them. Silently he offered up a prayer that he wasn't screwing up. He wanted a lifetime with Allie—white picket fence, two kids, a dog, the whole damn thing. A ménage with his best friend suddenly didn't seem to be the best way to achieve that goal.

"Dammit, man," Alex said, interrupting his distressing thoughts. "Stop thinking so hard."

Allie giggled and kissed first Alex then Charlie. Both kisses were quick but deep and passionate and full of unspoken promises. Charlie marveled at how the image of Allie kissing Alex was as seductive as the kiss she'd given him. Throwing up his hands in defeat, he laughed.

"You two win. Let's go home, Allie," he said as he wrapped an arm around her waist and led her out of the bar.

Chapter Two

Alex knew that Allie realized the enormity of what he was expecting, what he was hoping would evolve from this night. He'd frightened her six years earlier with his proposition and she'd left town. At the time, he'd thought she had run away from him, from the knowledge that he wanted to share her with Charlie. That he wanted her to share Anderson with him. But now that she was back, he wondered if that had been the case at all. Unlike Ginny, Allie had never been content to remain at home when her mother's health and the family's financial woes made attending college an impossibility.

Alex realized that over the past six years she'd accomplished at least some of her goals—seeing the world, experiencing a multitude of amazing adventures, flexing her wings and finding herself. He prayed her return home meant she was ready to explore the next horizon with them—sharing her deepest, darkest sexual desires.

They retrieved Charlie's keys from the valet but waved the man off when he offered to pull the vehicle around, opting instead to get it themselves. When they reached the passenger door of Charlie's truck, Alex gripped Allie's arm, spinning her around and pressing her against the cool metal.

"Panties," he said, holding out his hand.

Her face flushed at his demand, but he knew better than to believe she was embarrassed. He knew her, knew all about her taste for adventure, the steamy passion that drove her. She was perfect for them, and Alex had suspected it for years.

He'd made a miscalculation, a terrible mistake in approaching her that night by the bonfire. She'd been too young, too inexperienced. But finally he'd have a chance to make up for lost time.

Charlie came to stand beside him and he knew his friend's move was premeditated. They were shielding her from anyone who might be in the parking lot. She reached down and slowly peeled the poorest excuse for panties he'd ever seen down her long, luscious legs. She handed him the damp material and Alex grinned. Oh yeah, she was ready to roll.

He glanced over at Charlie and felt a deep sense of unease. He'd always thought Allie would be the easy one to convince to participate in this unusual triangle, so when she'd left town, he'd shied away from pursuing Charlie the way he'd wanted to. He simply couldn't run the risk of pushing away another person he cared about.

Now he knew his feelings for Charlie were as strong as they'd ever been and, with Allie's return, it felt as if the pieces were falling into place. Unfortunately Charlie had no idea how far Alex wanted to push this ménage. It wasn't just a bit of sexual experimenting in Alex's mind but something much, much more.

He looked back at Allie and smiled. There was time to explore all of that later. Tonight he was determined to prove to the wild woman in front of him that he loved her and wanted her. While he suspected Charlie was only just realizing the depths of his own feelings for Allie, Alex had known all along how much he cared for her.

He bent down and lightly brushed her lips with a soft kiss. Her arms wrapped around his shoulders and she pulled him closer, attempting to deepen the kiss. She'd never be fully dominated in the bedroom, and Alex had no doubt she'd attempt to direct their lovemaking every bit as much as he or Charlie. Hell, probably more.

Christ, three alphas should make for some interesting foreplay. She was no wallflower, no shrinking violet. She was a hot-blooded temptress and Alex was starving for her.

"Save some of that for me." Charlie's voice drifted over them from behind, and Alex released her and watched as she offered his friend the same heated, passionate kiss. As the kiss deepened and Charlie's hands began kneading her breasts, Alex realized they were walking a fine line and they'd be hard-pressed to get the woman home if they didn't leave now.

"Get in the car," Alex said when Charlie and Allie broke apart for a moment. Charlie nodded, realizing the urgency, and quickly walked around to the driver's side. Alex opened the passenger door and helped Allie into the truck before climbing in after her. Once they were all inside, Alex turned to her.

"Lift up your skirt, Allie. Let us see that hot pussy of yours."

"I'll show you mine if you show me yours," she challenged.

Charlie laughed. "You're a wild one, Allie-cat. Seems like you might need a bit of taming."

Allie shrugged playfully at his threat. "Oh you boys are welcome to try, but I have to warn you, I'm a helluva lot more fun when I'm being bad."

"I'll bet you are," Alex said. "Fine, you're on." As he spoke, he unbuttoned his jeans and jerked down his zipper, pulling out his painfully hard erection. Allie's tongue darted out to moisten her lower lip as she watched, and Alex was overwhelmed with the impulse to pull her head down and beg her to lick his cock.

"Your turn." At Charlie's words, Alex glanced over. His friend had taken out his own hard-on and was working the turgid flesh with his fist. Alex had to fight back a groan of desire at the image of his friend pleasuring himself, afraid of how Charlie would respond to it.

“Mmmm,” Allie hummed. “Yummy.”

“You have no idea. Now be a good naughty girl and pull up that skirt,” Charlie demanded. The rough tone of his voice combined with the dominant streak Alex knew his friend possessed had his own cock rising and reaching critical mass in an instant. Shit, he’d never last until they got home.

Allie lifted her hips and slowly dragged the lacy material up to her waist. Without her panties, there was just enough light provided by a streetlamp to expose Alex to heaven on earth.

“Jesus,” he muttered. “You’re shaved.” Alex couldn’t for the life of him understand how that fact had escaped his notice in the bar. He’d been so focused on Allie—and how Charlie would respond to his touching her—he’d failed to enjoy the moment fully himself. Well, he’d make up for that now.

Charlie’s hand beat his to Allie’s hot cunt, and Alex fought against coming at the sight of his friend driving his thick finger inside her. Allie cried out at the rough touch, and Alex decided it wouldn’t take much more to push her into an orgasm. Charlie’s hand stilled and Alex glanced up, surprised to find his friend’s gaze on him.

"Both of us. Just like in the bar," Charlie said softly, and Alex nodded.

They'd both enjoy feeling her first orgasm. They were going to bring Allie over together. The comprehension that everything he'd wanted for so long was finally happening left Alex light-headed.

He added his finger, relishing the feeling of Allie's hot juices and Charlie's strong hand beside his. With his free hand, he mimicked Charlie's movements, rubbing his own cock firmly. He fought the impulse to reach over and give Charlie a hand job he wouldn't soon forget. Taking a deep breath, he forced himself to be patient.

They moved their fingers in unison inside her as Allie whimpered and thrust her hips against their touch. Alex was shocked when he felt Allie's hand close over his. Looking up, he saw she'd done the same to Charlie and, as they fucked her with their fingers, she worked her fists along their cocks.

He wouldn't last long. Her hot cunt, her hand on his cock and the image of Charlie and Allie teetering on the precipice of orgasm pushed him to the edge.

"Fuck," he gritted out. "I can't hold back. I'm coming."

His explosion seemed to break the silent tension in all of them, and Allie screamed with her climax, as semen erupted from the end of Charlie's cock in great, long spurts.

When he came back to earth, Alex saw Charlie kissing Allie, heard him murmuring sweet nothings, calming her before he looked up at him.

"That was fucking amazing," Charlie said with a crooked grin, and Alex burst into laughter.

"I think it was actually amazing fucking," he corrected, and Allie giggled.

"Charlie, start this damn truck and get us home so the three of us can take a shower and amaze the fuck out of each other again," she teased.

Charlie peeled the tires in his rush to get them home.

* * *

As they pulled into the driveway, Alex watched as Charlie lifted Allie out of the truck and carried her to the front porch of their house. He couldn't hold back a grin as he listened to Allie's demands to be put down while Charlie ignored her. For over a decade, he'd watched the two people he loved most in the world dance around each other as if afraid to touch, afraid to admit what he'd always known.

The three of them were a set, meant to belong to each other in a completely unconventional way.

Allie knew what he'd wanted when she'd left. His feelings hadn't changed and she clearly knew that by coming to their home with both of them, she was accepting his offer. He'd begun to give up hope that she would ever come back to them, afraid she simply couldn't tolerate what he was asking.

Glancing back at him, Charlie raised his eyebrows in question. Alex grinned and shook his keys at him. Tonight, he wanted both of them in his bed. He unlocked the door to his side of the duplex. Charlie set Allie down inside the front door, and Alex walked over to her, taking her face in his hands. "Tonight is about you, hellion. Just you."

She glanced over her shoulder at Charlie before looking back at him with a questioning glance. Alex knew she was recalling his confession about Anderson, but he wanted—no, needed—her to understand that he loved her as well. His feelings for her had nothing to do with his feelings for Charlie Anderson.

Charlie stepped up behind her and wrapped his arms around her waist. Alex could see her nipples harden at the contact, poking through the thin material of her sexy blouse. "We won't force this on you, Allie. The decision is yours," Alex added.

He watched Charlie's grip on Allie tighten, and he could sense how badly his friend wanted this. Any reservations he'd suffered in the bar seemed to have been dismissed.

"You're not getting rid of me that easily," she whispered lightly, and Alex felt the vise that had been gripping his heart since she'd returned home loosen and fall away. She would accept both of them into her bed and her body and, with any luck, after tonight, she would accept them both into her life—forever.

"How about that shower?" Alex suggested.

"I thought you'd never ask," she teased.

As Alex led them through his house, he was struck by the utter rightness of this moment. He'd fallen in love with Allie Brooks when she was sixteen. At the time, life at her house had been falling apart and she'd run away from home.

Her mother had been diagnosed with cancer, and her older sister Ginny had given up her dream of attending college to stay home and care for her. He and Anderson had been packing up, getting ready to head off to college when Ginny called to say they couldn't find Allie…

Alex and Anderson had driven around for hours before finally spotting her climbing into a truck with a rather rough-looking character outside an all-night diner.

"Get outta that damn truck," Alex growled as he grabbed Allie from the piece-of-shit Ford.

"What the hell do you think you're doing?" she yelled. She struggled not to fall on the gravel as Alex pulled her out and Charlie reached over to support her until she found her footing.

"What the fuck?" the driver cursed, opening his door and coming around the truck. "Who the fuck are you two?"

"We're the guys who are gonna kick your ass and then call the cops!" Charlie yelled.

"Oh yeah, what for?"

"For kidnapping a minor," Charlie spat.

"Minor?" the asshole asked, turning to look at Allie. "You told me you were eighteen."

Allie shrugged belligerently. Since her mother had been diagnosed with cancer, Alex had watched Allie fall further and further into self-destructive behavior. Her pride in her appearance had disappeared and rather than the clean-cut, pretty girl next door he'd grown up with, she'd turned into the Goth queen from hell.

"She's sixteen," Alex answered as the man's eyes narrowed.

"Fuck, man. I didn't know. Lying bitch said she wanted a ride to the next town."

Charlie's fist flew and connected with the bastard's jaw before Alex could jump in and hold him back.

"Don't call her a bitch!" Charlie shouted.

"Cool it, Anderson! Just get Allie and let's go."

The man looked as if he wanted to retaliate for the punch, but taking a closer look at the two young men ready to take him on, he seemed to reconsider.

"Fuck this shit. I'm outta here." He got back in his truck and stomped on the gas, throwing gravel back at them in his rush to get out of the secluded parking lot.

Allie whirled on them in anger, but Alex was unwilling to hear any of the poison she seemed ready to spew. She'd nearly left town with that asshole. God only knew what would have happened if they hadn't found her. "Don't say a word!" he shouted. "Your sister is out of her mind worrying about you. You were supposed to be home hours ago."

"Oh no, Ginny the good daughter is upset! Gosh, I really do feel bad now." Her words dripped with sarcasm. She'd been driving all of them crazy with her reckless behavior lately.

"You little smartass," Alex muttered. "You're acting like a spoiled, selfish princess."

"Fuck you, Taylor!" she cried out.

"What's going on inside that pretty head of yours, Allie?" Charlie asked softly.

She sucked in a breath at Charlie's kind question, and Alex could see she obviously hadn't expected tenderness. Tears formed in her eyes before she turned away from them, and Alex cursed his own harsh words.

"I'm not going home and you two can't make me," she whispered.

"Oh we can't, huh?" Alex asked, more than prepared to throw her ass in the car if she took one step in the wrong direction.

"This is none of your business! Shouldn't you two be packing for college? Go away and leave me alone."

"No," Alex answered simply. "Get in the car."

"I…I can't go home." She turned and looked at Charlie, ignoring him. Alex knew she wasn't quite sure what to make of him, and he suspected deep down she preferred Charlie to him. "Please, Anderson. I c-can't go home."

"Why not?" his friend asked.

She looked down at the ground.

"Allie, why not?" He repeated Charlie's question, concern and worry overwhelming him.

Tears sprung to her eyes and angry, pain-laced words flew from her in such a rush, he struggled to understand her. "I can't watch it anymore! God, I'm not strong like Ginny. I never have been. I can't watch my mother die! I can't stay in that house and hear her crying from the pain or throwing up because of that fucking chemotherapy. I can't watch my dad and Ginny act like she's getting better when I know she's not!"

She turned away from them for a moment, and Alex could see her shoulders shaking as she tried to choke back the sobs building in her slight frame.

When she turned back around, the previous pain in her gaze had been replaced with unadulterated rage. "She's fucking dying! I know it! They think I'm a goddamn kid and that I can't figure out the truth! They whisper about her diagnosis and shut up every time I come in the room. Do they think I'm stupid? Do they think I can't see?"

Alex felt her words in his gut. In their attempts to protect Allie—the baby—her family had left her alone, confused and forced to draw her own conclusions about her mother's illness.

"Allie," Charlie whispered. "She's not dying. Your mom is fighting the cancer and she has a good chance, a real good chance of beating it."

"God, Anderson. Stop lying to me! I can't stand this anymore. I just want somebody to tell me the fucking truth!"

Charlie started to respond but Alex moved forward first. He reached out and gripped her shoulders, shaking her. "Anderson's not lying. Your mom is fighting—hard. Just today the doctor said the treatment is working. There's a good chance her cancer will go into remission. I'm sorry they've been hiding things from you, but I wouldn't lie to you—ever. You know that."

She didn't fight his grip and looked at him closely. He suspected she was trying to read the veracity of his words in his face.

"Remission? She's not dying?"

He smiled and shook his head. "Like mother, like daughter. Both of you are too headstrong and stubborn to ever give in to anyone or anything."

She smiled at his comment before gasping back a relieved sob and looking at Charlie. “Swear to me. Swear he isn’t lying to me.”

Charlie moved forward and took her cheeks in his hands, holding her face gently in his grasp. “I would never lie to you, Allie, and neither would Taylor. Your mom’s a fighter, just like you. She’ll beat this, I know it.”

Charlie pulled her forward and placed a soft kiss on her forehead and the image of it knocked Alex back a step. He struggled with the sudden awareness that there was something innately different about this girl, something special that he couldn’t quite put his finger on.

Now as she followed them down the hall, Alex knew exactly what it was. Had known for some time. She was their woman. She belonged to him and Charlie, and all he had to do was convince them both to take a chance on what he’d felt in his heart for years.

“Wow,” Allie breathed when they walked into Alex’s bathroom. He grinned at her response.

He’d created the space with the three of them in mind. There was a large, open walk-in shower that filled nearly half the room with not just two showerheads but three. There were benches in all four corners and plenty of room for the three lovers to experiment. On the other side of the room was an oversized Jacuzzi tub and along the center wall were double sinks, above which hung a huge mirror and recessed lighting.

"I think I'd like to take back my previous comments about the extravagance of your bathroom," Charlie said with a crooked grin.

"Oh, so now you get it," Alex teased as he recalled Charlie trying to convince him when they were building the house that such a bathroom was a waste of money.

Allie giggled and hastily began to strip off her clothing. "You'd both be getting it if you'd hurry up and undress."

Her words hit their mark as Alex quickly unbuttoned and pulled off his shirt. He wondered if they'd ever be able to approach the act of lovemaking without dashing through everything. He knew they should be building up the anticipation of the moment, undressing each other, tantalizing and teasing, but he couldn't see past the unleashed need that was clawing away at him, demanding that he take her now.

Once he'd shed the rest of his clothing, he stepped into the shower and turned on the water, adjusting the heat level until steam began to rise. Turning, he saw that Charlie and Allie were also naked and his friend was kissing her as if his life depended on it. Alex stood beneath the jets of water for several moments, watching as Charlie's hands worshipped Allie's body and his lips paid homage to her mouth, her cheeks, her ears.

One drunken night, Charlie had cried about Allie's leaving. He knew his friend, too far gone at the time, didn't recall the conversation. But it had torn Alex apart to know how deeply Charlie had been hurt by Allie's departure—and to realize that it had been his words, his desires that had driven her away.

Shaking away the unsavory memory, Alex reached out to pull the couple into the shower. "Too much more of that and we're going to run out of hot water before you two ever make it in here."

Allie smiled and took his outstretched hand, letting him lead her under the pulsing jets. "Oh," she sighed. "That feels wonderful."

Charlie joined them, moving to stand behind Allie as Alex took his turn with her lovely lips. Alex felt Charlie's hands caressing her body, and every now and then his fingers, his knuckles, would brush against Alex's chest. He tried to still the overwhelming impact Charlie's accidental touches fired in his body.

Allie pulled back from the kiss to look at him, and Alex was amazed to see total understanding and compassion in her gaze. "Soon," she breathed against his mouth as she drew him back into her kisses.

Chapter Three

Allie reached for the bottle of shower gel sitting on a ledge and marveled over the fact she was truly here with Alex and Charlie. Over the years she'd thought of them almost obsessively. Worried she'd made the wrong choice by leaving. Fearful she'd thrown away her one chance at happiness with them.

Jim used to tease her constantly about her fantasies, and she grinned as she considered the fact that only her boss would think her regrets funny. Jim was constantly amused by her remorse over losing out on the opportunity to explore a committed ménage. She'd fallen into depression and threatened to come home more than a few times during the past six years, but every time, Jim would whisk her off to Italy or Switzerland or someplace where the scenery would leave her breathless, convincing her that she wasn't ready, that it was too soon. And he never failed to prove his point that she'd made the right decision.

She'd needed to find herself and now, as she stood between them, Alex and Charlie engulfing her with their strong, sexy bodies, she knew she was offering them a whole woman, one with no regrets or unfulfilled dreams.

Well, other than the one I'm experiencing at the moment. She giggled lightly at the thought.

"What's so funny?" Charlie whispered in her ear, nipping at the lobe while pinching her nipples so firmly she dropped the bottle of shower gel.

She moaned at the intensity of his touches and instantly forgot his question.

Alex ran his hands over her hips, pulling her closer to him. His erection brushed against her stomach as he bent down to kiss her lips before murmuring against them, "You didn't answer Charlie's question." His hands drifted to her pussy and his fingers toyed with her clit.

She sucked in an excited breath. "Um. What was his question?"

Charlie chuckled. "You were smiling, laughing. Why?"

She looked over her shoulder at the face of her teenage crush and giggled again. "I'm just so happy. It sort of keeps slipping out."

Charlie smiled widely at her words. "Oh I like that. I think we're going to have to see if we can squeeze more of those giggles out." As he spoke, he roughly pinched her nipples as Alex drove a finger into her drenched opening. She gasped loudly at the overwhelming impact of both men touching her, teasing her, driving her too quickly to orgasm. She'd barely recovered from the one in the truck, and yet she suspected she'd be screaming in seconds.

Alex pulled his finger out, only to return with another. "I like the giggles," he said as he thrust roughly inside her several times. She reached for his shoulders, clinging to them for support as her climax started. Charlie pinched her nipples again and she screamed, her body shuddering as she fell headfirst into the powerful orgasm.

For several moments none of them moved, as the hot jets of water pounded against their bodies. Allie struggled and gasped to fill her lungs with air, besieged by the glorious sensations attacking her body. Her skin suddenly felt too sensitive, too cognizant of every drop of water, every brush of their rough fingers, every hot breath from their lips.

"I like the giggles," Alex repeated, rousing her from her sex-induced stupor. "But I love the screams more."

"Oh yeah," Charlie agreed. "I think maybe I would rather hear a few more of those tonight."

"Tonight?" she asked weakly, trying to work up the energy to be offended when both men laughed.

"We're not finished yet, Allie. Nowhere near, in fact." Alex cupped her cheeks and kissed her, lightly, softly, and yet it was enough to set her overheated body on fire again.

"I think you lost something," Charlie said as he bent down to retrieve the shower gel she'd dropped earlier. She took it from him and struggled to force strength into her still-trembling limbs. She poured some of the sweet-smelling soap into her palm and reached over to rub the lather onto Alex's chest while Charlie continued to stroke her breasts from behind.

Never in her wildest dreams would she have imagined the beauty, the intensity of being so close to these two men. They'd starred in all her young woman fantasies, but now she feared her heart would burst at the excitement of having them both so near, touching her, loving her.

Alex bent down and placed another seductive kiss on her lips, and she melted at the contact. Charlie's arms tightened around her, and she wondered how much of her weight her legs were supporting and how much Charlie was. His strength mesmerized her, and her body's fluids ran rampant down her leg.

She turned slowly, pouring out more of the gel, using it to lather Charlie's chest as well. While Alex's upper body was completely bare, Charlie had a light dusting of soft hair around his rock-hard pecs. She ran her fingers through it as she massaged the gel into his skin. Alex used the lather on his torso to soap up her back, moving his body slowly back and forth against hers as his cock nestled between the crack of her ass.

She shook her head slightly, willing herself to remain cognizant, in control. She refused to take another moment's pleasure from them without returning a bit of it. They'd been so attentive, so amazingly sexy.

For the third time she added more gel to her hand, reaching down to use the soap on Charlie's thick member. He hissed at her touch and she felt Alex stop moving. She could feel his gaze on her hand as she lightly caressed Charlie's cock. Charlie's eyes had drifted closed when she'd gripped him, and Allie could feel the tension in Alex's body grow as she slicked her fist up and down.

She knew Alex's feelings toward Charlie hadn't changed, and she'd wondered several times since she'd returned home if the men had succumbed to them. After all, they had built a house together. It was her conversations with Ginny that had convinced her Alex hadn't confessed his feelings to his best friend, and she couldn't begin to fathom how he'd hidden his love for so long.

She'd thought long and hard about Alex's comments by the bonfire over the past few years and she knew, deep in her heart, that she wanted Charlie and Alex. She could understand and sympathize with Alex's desires, his needs—because she shared them. Right or wrong, she didn't have a doubt she could give her heart and soul to both these men in an instant.

Turning her head slightly, she watched Alex's eyes follow the movement of her hand and a delightfully sinful idea crossed her mind. It might be too soon, but she worried there was also such a thing as too late. She deliberately lightened her grip, softened her strokes.

Charlie's eyes drifted open, and she saw a touch of confusion in the depths of his lovely blue orbs. She'd obviously proven in the truck that she knew how to do this the right way.

"Am I doing it wrong?" the devil prompted her to ask with an innocent whisper.

"Harder," Charlie answered, his hands on her hips, gripping her tightly. "You don't have to be afraid you'll hurt me."

She tightened her grip, but this time only moved a couple of inches along his shaft, never touching the top or bottom, merely massaging the middle. She could sense both men's frustrations growing.

"Show me," she whispered to Alex. Charlie's body stiffened at her words—but Allie couldn't help noticing his cock did too.

"Allie," Alex breathed against her cheek. She knew he meant to refuse her, so she halted his words, instead reaching for his hand and placing it atop hers on Charlie's cock.

Both men sucked in a breath at the contact, even though Alex wasn't actually touching Charlie, but rather resting his hand on top of hers.

She looked at Alex and softly repeated her request. "Show me how." As she spoke, she smiled and watched Alex return it. He bent down to press a soft kiss on her cheek then turned his gaze to their clasped hands.

"Harder," he said, his voice so gruff with emotion he had to clear his throat. "Like this." He tightened his grip on her hand and Charlie moaned. "And you need to move your hand all the way along his shaft. Like this." He moved their hands, Allie's still slick with gel, from the base of Charlie's cock to the tip. Up and down they moved as Charlie closed his eyes and groaned.

"Jesus, that feels good," he said as Allie and Alex continued their rough, loving caresses. On one upward move, Alex ran his finger along the tip of Charlie's cock, playing with the slit, rubbing in the pre-cum he found there for only a second or two.

Allie suspected he'd forgotten himself for a moment because when Charlie's eyes flew open and landed on his, Alex stopped, his finger still poised over the tip. They all stood motionless for seemingly endless moments.

Anxious to keep things moving in a forward motion, Allie repeated Alex's touch and Charlie sucked in a breath. "Like that?" she asked, as if Alex had been sharing another secret of the male anatomy.

She felt rather than saw Alex nodding behind her. Charlie's gaze never left Alex's, and she worried that she'd gone too far, too fast in pushing for this. Refusing to lose any ground, she reached back and cupped Alex's balls with her free hand while forcing Alex to continue his lesson on Charlie. Both men moved at her touch and Charlie chuckled. The tension of the moment seemed to pass.

"Ever get the feeling she's trying to play the top?" Charlie asked.

Allie was perfectly familiar with the term and started to inform him that she wasn't merely playing. Unfortunately, Alex answered first.

"We'll soon have that little flaw in her character corrected." He replied with such cockiness Allie couldn't resist giving his balls an extra-hard squeeze. Alex hissed and gripped her wrist firmly. "Easy with the crown jewels, hellion," he warned.

"Easy with the caveman comments, Alex Taylor. Seems to me there are plenty of roles to go around in this little trio of ours."

Charlie grinned at her words, his hands drifting from her hips to her waist. "Can we divvy up the parts after this shower? My cock is about to explode."

Alex looked at his friend guiltily, and Allie felt him pull her hand along Charlie's cock again. The force of his movement and tight grip stunned her, and she thought for sure they must be hurting Charlie. She glanced up, concerned, until she realized he was about to come. Rather than pain, she saw complete concentration and bliss as he began to thrust into their joined hands.

"Fuck, I'm coming!" Charlie muttered as his cock erupted, his semen shooting out. Alex never loosened their shared grip and directed the jets of his friend's seed so that it landed on Allie's stomach.

"Holy shit!" Charlie exclaimed as he opened his eyes. He watched as Alex rubbed his semen into her skin. "Christ, man."

Alex laughed and Allie was overwhelmed by the sound of pure joy in it. He'd given them both so much, but the brush of his thick, hard shaft against her back reminded her that he hadn't found his own pleasure.

She turned quickly, catching the surprise in Alex's face as she went to her knees and engulfed the head of his cock in her mouth.

"Dammit, Allie," he breathed out as she slowly worked her way down his hard flesh. He was thicker than any man she'd ever seen, and she wondered if perhaps she hadn't bitten off more than she could chew…literally. Charlie's hands drifted to her shoulders, and she wished she could see what was going on above her head. Practically kneeling between Alex's legs, with Charlie snug behind her, Allie knew the men were positioned close to each other—perhaps uncomfortably so—and she wondered how Charlie was reacting to that fact.

"Think I owe you one," she heard Charlie mutter before he knelt down next to her. Her mind reeled as Alex's hands found their way to her hair, gripping tightly. She could sense a slight tremble in his fingers and had no doubt he was amazed by his friend's actions as well. Charlie's face was next to hers, and she heard his voice in her ear.

"Try to loosen your jaw, Allie-cat. He's big, but you can take him in."

She tried to follow Charlie's commands. She knew how to open her throat, how to swallow a man's cock, but part of her was worried about accomplishing the feat with Alex's wide girth—and Charlie watching so closely.

Charlie's hand drifted down her stomach, and she felt his featherlight touch against her clit. "Follow my directions and you'll be rewarded," he prompted, rubbing her clit more firmly. She gasped at the touch and felt a bit more of Alex's cock glide into her mouth.

"Good girl," Charlie muttered. Out of the corner of her eye, she could see him glance up at Alex. "Seems our lady just needs the proper motivation."

Allie started to pull back to tell Charlie Anderson just where he and his motivation could get off, but Alex's grip on her head held her in place.

"Shhh," Alex soothed. "You can kick his ass later," he joked. "Right now I need you to suck my cock."

Allie remembered how much Alex had given her and moved forward again, taking another inch into her mouth. As promised, Charlie rubbed her clit hard, the touch divine.

She started to work Alex's cock in earnest, his hands on her head and Charlie's directions guiding her through the hottest blowjob she'd ever given. She was dripping wet, but all she wanted was Alex's come. She wanted to give him an earth-shattering orgasm like the ones he'd rocked her world with tonight. Surprisingly, she suspected she was going to be sharing in what she'd intended to be a gift for him.

Charlie's fingers continued to tease, tantalize, tempt and taunt her clit until she felt as if her heart would burst at the impact of so many sensations pummeling her at once. The taste of Alex's arousal, the sound of Charlie's mesmerizing voice in her ear and the feel of his hands on her body, the image of these two men loving her, loving each other even if they didn't realize it yet, surrounded her.

She heard Alex's moan begin deep in his chest, and she engulfed him in her throat one last time as he erupted. She drank him down, feeling a twinge of regret when he pulled free. Her feeling of loss, of emptiness, lasted only until Charlie drove three fingers into her weeping pussy. She climaxed immediately, screaming in ecstasy at the unexpected touch.

Her eyes drifted closed as she felt herself being lifted from the floor of the shower. She heard the water turn off and the murmur of two deep voices beside her, although she was too exhausted to understand the words. Soft sheets and a fluffy pillow were the last things she remembered as she fell into a deep and dreamless sleep.

Chapter Four

Allie tiptoed into Alex's kitchen, praying she would find coffee there. She was not a morning person and without her jumpstart of java, she was absolutely useless. She'd been pleased to wake and discover herself smack-dab in the middle of two lovely men. Lucky thing Alex owned a king-sized bed. She'd carefully extricated herself from between them, thrown on one of Alex's T-shirts and left them sound asleep. Poor babies looked exhausted. She giggled as she recalled the hottest shower she'd ever taken in her life then marveled over the fact they hadn't even had actual sex yet.

She was humming softly to herself and quietly sipping her second cup of coffee, when she felt someone's gaze on her. She glanced up to find Charlie, dressed in nothing but his dress pants from the previous night, leaning in the doorway, watching her. She fought back the instinct to drool at his six-pack abs.

"Why did you run off with Jim Griffin?" he asked.

"Where the hell did that question come from?" Allie was shocked by Charlie's conversation topic.

"Why, Allie?"

She looked at his face and saw such a perfect mixture of sadness and confusion, she wasn't sure how to respond. She shrugged. "I don't know what you want me to say."

"He was old enough to be your father. Hell, he was your father's friend. One minute you're happy at home and the next minute you're gallivanting all over the world with the guy. What the hell was he to you?"

Allie took a deep breath, trying to calm her suddenly racing heart. How could she explain her decision without hurting his feelings, without seeming like a selfish, heartless bitch?

"Charlie, I was never happy at home. You know that."

He scowled at her response, and she knew he was remembering the night he'd caught her running away.

"You seemed happy to me once your mother started to recover. Did a pretty good impersonation of it.

"How the hell do you know if I was happy or not?" She couldn't contain the sudden anger at his words. "You weren't here, Charlie. You were off at college, drinking your way through fraternity parties and fucking yourself silly with sorority sisters. You weren't here. You have no idea how I felt."

Charlie's own fury escaped and he shouted at her, frustration clear in every word. "Was I supposed to be here? Is that what you wanted? We weren't dating. We weren't a couple. Shit, you were still in high school!"

She shook her head, cursing herself for her harsh words. He didn't deserve her anger.

"No. You were exactly where you were supposed to be. I'm just saying that you can't stand here and try to tell me that I was happy. Unless you have some mind-reading ability that I don't know about, you really have no idea how I felt."

Charlie shrugged and nodded. "So you were unhappy. That doesn't explain Griffin."

Allie grinned guiltily and shrugged. "I guess you could say he saved me."

Charlie turned away from her, crossing the room to pour himself a cup of coffee, and she could see from the stiffness in his shoulders that her answer had clearly pissed him off. "Saved you from what?" he muttered so quietly she almost didn't hear him.

"I don't know," she admitted. "From myself. From my restlessness, my recklessness. I don't think I can put this into words that you'll understand."

"Try," he said, turning back to face her. His anger seemed to have faded as quickly as hers, and she could see he was willing to hear her out, regardless of the fact he might not like what she was going to say.

"I'm not like Ginny," she said softly. "She's a homebody and a creature of comfort. When my mother was diagnosed with cancer, Ginny never blinked twice at the thought of giving up college and staying home to help take care of her." Allie took a deep breath, her next words too painful to admit. "I didn't. I wish I'd been able…"

"You didn't feel the same," Charlie finished for her, walking to the table and reaching over to take her hand in his.

"I'm a terrible daughter. A horrible person, I know that." Allie swallowed hard against the lump in her throat and tried to blink away the tears filling her eyes.

"No you're not."

"Oh please, don't bother saying any differently. My mother was dying of cancer and all I could think of was escaping, getting the hell away from here."

"So you'll never be a nurse," Charlie teased, and Allie smiled at his jest.

"It was more than running from my mother's disease. I had this fire inside me, this ache that wouldn't go away. I was so afraid that I would never see more than the twenty square miles of this shithole town and that I'd die of old age in my parents' house. Hell, I was terrified I'd die in my childhood bedroom surrounded by fucking posters of Leonardo DiCaprio and Brad Pitt."

"Don't forget New Kids on the Block," Charlie joked. "I seem to recall you had an abundance of those guys hanging on your walls."

Allie laughed. "Don't remind me. Oh, Charlie, there was just so much I wanted to see, to do…to experience."

"And you couldn't do that if you were tied to home. But your mother—"

"Recovered," Allie finished. "Yes, she did. Her cancer went into remission and all was well with the world. Problem was, I'd graduated from high school, taken a shitty job as a waitress and I was still consumed by this damn impatience that told me there was more to life, more to see."

"So what happened?"

"I was waiting tables at the diner. Jim had become a regular customer after his wife died, and we spent a lot of time talking about our lives, our ambitions. It's strange how much we had in common given the fact my life was really just starting while his seemed to be winding down. One night we started listing all the things we wanted to see, things we wanted to do before we died. We ended up talking until the diner closed. Turned out we shared the same sort of wanderlust. Next thing I know, Jim decided to make our dreams a reality. He offered me a job. I took it and, well…you know the rest." She stumbled over her half-truth, fully aware of how much of the tale she'd omitted.

"No, I don't know," Charlie said shortly. "According to Ginny, you were his personal assistant, but since he didn't have a damn job, what exactly were you assisting him with?"

Allie could tell from his tone what he was thinking—and she couldn't refute his claims.

"Do you want to know if I slept with Jim?" she asked hotly. "Yeah, Charlie, I did. So there. Are you happy? Did you get the nitty-gritty details you were looking for?"

"Your father—" he started.

"Would blow a gasket if he ever found out about the sex," she interrupted. "And yeah, he wasn't too thrilled with one of his friends dragging his youngest daughter through what he called 'Jim's midlife crisis' at first, either. But after a while he stopped worrying about it and just accepted it."

"Christ, Allie. He was too old for you."

"Who says? Why does age make a difference—or anything else, for that matter? It's what's on the inside that counts, the rest is just wrapping paper."

He shook his head, his look a perfect combination of frustration and anger. "Were you sleeping with him when you left?" he asked.

"No, I wasn't. Shit, Charlie, what's with this third degree? You got the answer you were looking for. I fucked Jim Griffin—loads of times. So what? And you wanna know something else? I loved it. I loved him!"

She sucked back a breath at the sobs threatening to consume her. She'd missed Jim terribly since his passing, but she felt strongly that grief was a private thing, and there was no way she'd break down in front of Charlie, despite her anger over the third degree.

"I'm sorry," he said softly, pulling her up and enveloping her in his embrace. His compassion and the genuine sorrow in his voice caught her unaware, and she felt the tears she'd kept locked away since Jim's death break free.

"Damn you," she said as she tried to stop crying. "Why does any of this matter? Why bring up all this ancient history?"

"It's my fault." Alex's voice drifted to them from across the room.

Allie jerked out of Charlie's embrace, surprised to find Alex in the doorway. Like Charlie, he'd only half dressed and was wearing a pair of tatty jeans. How long had he been listening to their conversation?

"What?" she asked.

"It was my fault you left. I pressured you that night by the bonfire, Allie. You were still young and I asked you for way more than you were ready to give," Alex replied.

"What did you say that night?" Charlie asked, and Allie could feel the walls closing in on them. The happiness of the previous night vanishing with the accusations, the jealousy, the suspicions. How could they have fallen so far, so fast? When she'd woken up this morning, she'd felt years younger and lighter than air. She hated drudging through the past, especially when none of it mattered.

"He said he wanted a ménage. Between the three of us," Allie replied. "But that's not why I left town."

"Sure it's not," Alex answered sarcastically.

Allie raised her eyebrows at him and grinned. "I wanted both of you even then, Alex. I really did. But dammit, I knew what would happen if I gave in to that desire."

"What would have happened?" Alex asked, and she sensed he was relieved by her words, if not wholly convinced.

"I would have stayed. I would have ended up in bed with both of you and it would have been wonderful and terrible at the same time."

"Why?" Charlie asked.

"Because I had too much I wanted to experience, to do. I wanted you, but if I'd given in to the attraction, the passion, I would never have gone off on my own. I would have let myself be sucked into your lives and I would still be working in that damn diner and dreaming of far-off places and reckless adventures. Staying here would have killed me."

"We would have taken you places, Allie. Let you experience all those things." Charlie's words were sincere, yet Allie couldn't help the laugh of disbelief that flew from her lips.

"Ha! If I'd told you I wanted to bungee jump off a bridge, Charlie, what would you have said?"

His eyebrows furrowed, and she watched him struggle to give her an honest answer. "I'd have said it was too dangerous."

She giggled at his response and leaned forward to kiss him gently on the cheek. "That's exactly what you would have said, and I would have respected your feelings, and chances are very good I would have skipped the bungee jumping, even though I desperately wanted to try it. How do you feel about skydiving?"

Alex growled. "I would have let you go, but I would have strapped you to me."

Allie laughed at his confession. "I went solo several times and it was exhilarating."

"Don't say any more," Charlie said quickly. "I have more than enough gray hair from just hearing Ginny read your letters over the years. I don't think I wanna hear firsthand accounts of every reckless, crazy, insane thing you did."

Allie shook her head, grinning. "I didn't think any of those things were insane. And I wouldn't change one second of the past six years."

"So Griffin let you do all that stuff?" Alex asked.

"I'd known Jim my whole life. He and my dad were good friends, but he changed after his wife died. They were married thirty years, and he'd spent the majority of his life working and accumulating a ridiculous pile of money. When Charlotte died, he realized he'd wasted all those years they'd spent together, worrying about trivial things like the mortgage and his firm, not enjoying their life together, their love.

"After we talked that night at the diner, he wanted to see some of those dreams fulfilled, and he wanted to give me the opportunity to enjoy them while I was young. So he sold his business and his house, bought the fancy sports car he'd always wanted and we hit the open road."

"And the bedroom," Charlie added. Allie could detect the slightest bit of resentment in his voice.

"We turned out to be kindred spirits in so many ways…and he really did hire me initially to be his personal assistant. At the time we'd left town, he'd been on his own for nearly a year. He was tired of being alone. It was my job to make the arrangements for hotels, airline tickets and so on and, in exchange, he paid the bills."

"Christ, I can understand why you called it a dream job in your letters to Brooks," Alex admitted.

"It would have definitely been a hard offer to turn down, and my position with Jim, our relationship, was perfectly platonic the first few years," Allie continued.

"But it was hard not to love him. He was handsome, charming, intelligent."

"You fell in love with him," Charlie said softly, but Allie shook her head.

"No, I don't think I did. I loved him dearly, but I wasn't in love with him and he wasn't in love with me. His heart belonged to Charlotte—always." She took a deep breath and decided if they were after truth, she'd give it all to them. "We had sex, but our relationship wasn't exclusive, and he certainly wasn't the only man I slept with these past six years."

Charlie and Alex's heads popped up at her words and Allie struggled to fight down her laugh. "Jesus, can you guys say 'double standard'? Have you both been choirboys your whole lives? Living chaste, pure lives and never touching women?"

Alex shrugged guiltily, and Allie knew she'd scored a point.

Charlie continued to scowl. "I don't want to know about your past love affairs," he barked. "Makes me want to kill every man who's ever looked at you."

"Including Alex?" she asked teasingly. Her question seemed to rock Charlie despite the fact she'd meant it as a joke.

"No," he admitted. "Not Alex."

His words were spoken quietly, and Allie could sense his confusion about the emotions his best friend seemed to evoke in him. She prayed she could help them both over the enormous hurdle they were facing. She had been in love with Charlie Anderson since she was in elementary school, and her feelings for Alex had definitely grown into more than mere friendship once they'd reached adulthood.

She'd decided a long time ago that she was in love with both of them and was so very grateful for the opportunity to share it with them. However, she wasn't sure how Charlie would respond to Alex's feelings toward him. Alex was obviously still head over heels in love with his best friend. Allie shook her head at the bizarre love triangle they formed.

Alex broke the uncomfortable silence that had fallen. "So how about some breakfast? I'm sure there must be some food in here somewhere."

Charlie shook his head. "Somehow I seriously doubt that. Stay here and I'll run over to my kitchen and grab some grub. You do own pans, don't you?"

Alex paused as if seriously considering the question before shrugging. "Hell if I know. What's a pan?" he joked.

Allie laughed. "Come on. Let's move this party to Charlie's kitchen. I'm dying to see this strange setup you guys call home."

Charlie grabbed her hand and started to tug her toward the front foyer, but she jerked back. "Shouldn't I throw on some clothes? Wouldn't want to give the neighbors an eyeful this early in the morning."

"We don't have any neighbors close enough to see our house," Charlie answered. Allie had suspected as much, but it had been dark when they'd arrived last night and she hadn't exactly been focused on what was outside the truck.

"Besides," Alex said, interrupting her thoughts, "we aren't going outside."

At the front entryway, Allie noticed a door she hadn't seen the night before. Charlie pulled it open and she was surprised to find herself in a mirror image of Alex's house. "We don't usually keep this door closed."

"If you guys wanted to keep on being roommates, why build the separate houses at all?" she asked.

"Well," Alex replied sheepishly, "sometimes a man needs his privacy."

Allie laughed at his response. "For sleepovers and such?"

Charlie shook his head and continued dragging her toward his kitchen. "I told you. We're not talking about that. I'm hungry."

"So I'm assuming by your fully stocked kitchen that most meals are consumed on this side of the duplex?" Allie asked as she watched Charlie open the fridge and begin pulling out bacon and eggs and sausage.

"I can't cook worth shit," Alex confessed. "Fortunately Charlie is a master in the kitchen."

Charlie grumbled at the comment. "He could learn if he wanted. Plays dumb so I have to do all the cooking."

Alex gave his friend a friendly punch on the arm. "Hey, I do the clean up, so it's not a completely one-sided deal. Plus I split the grocery bill. Don't make me out to sound like such a mooch."

Charlie dropped the food on the counter and grabbed a pan from a cabinet. "Think you can get a pot of coffee going, mooch?" he joked.

"You're cruising to get your ass kicked," Alex said as he reached for the coffee pot. Allie watched their easy camaraderie and grinned. She knew it would kill Charlie to hear her say it, but the two of them had been together so long they sounded a bit like an old married couple.

She sighed, feeling left out. Despite the fact they'd known her since she was nine, they shared a history she would never be a part of.

"What's wrong, Allie-cat?" Charlie asked.

She shook her head, unwilling to share her petty, envious thoughts. "Nothing. The kitchen looks like one of those places where the roles have already been assigned. There doesn't seem to be anything left for me to do."

Alex grinned evilly and she immediately regretted her remarks. "Oh, now I wouldn't say that's true." He approached her as he spoke, and Allie heard rather than saw Charlie coming toward her from behind.

"Alex," she said, lifting her finger in warning. Charlie's strong hands gripped her waist and before she could react, her T-shirt was pulled over her head, leaving her completely naked. She tried to grab the shirt out of Charlie's hand, but he flung it into the far corner of the room as Alex reached for her hips and turned her back toward him.

"What are you doing?" she asked as Alex nibbled sweetly at her throat.

"I was thinking you'd make a tasty appetizer," he murmured.

"That's funny," Charlie said from behind her, his hands enveloping her rear end, playing with the sensitive skin there. "I kind of fancied using this sexy body as a plate."

"If you think you're putting runny eggs on me and dipping your toast in it, you're nuts," she said, cursing her sudden breathlessness. Their hands were all over her and she was struggling to remain in control. Her body had surrendered itself to them completely last night, leaving her mind fighting futilely for a single foothold on sanity.

Strong hands lifted her onto the kitchen table, and Allie rejoiced in the idea of not having to support her weight any longer—until she felt herself being stretched out on the surface. Two hungry bears stared down at her and she wondered if they'd both been wrong.

She didn't feel like an appetizer or a plate—but rather suspected she was about to become the whole damn meal.

Chapter Five

Alex looked down at Allie spread across Charlie's kitchen table like a feast fit for the gods. After their heated session in the shower, all three of them had fallen asleep in his bed. As he studied Allie's curvy frame, he wondered how in the hell they'd managed to keep from actually having intercourse with her. One look at Charlie's face proved his friend was wondering the same thing.

"You look good enough to eat," he said, walking to where Allie's knees dangled over the edge.

Charlie remained by her side and bent down to suck one of Allie's tight nipples into his mouth. Allie gasped at Charlie's attack and Alex grinned. Years of being with his friend had proven to him that Charlie liked his sexual play with a rough edge to it. Spreading Allie's legs apart, he could see by the moisture pooling between them that she seemed to enjoy that fact.

"Yummy," he muttered as he leaned forward. He breathed in the scent of her sweet arousal, taking his time as he approached, savoring Allie's growing cries.

Obviously Charlie's ministrations to her breasts were pushing several hot buttons in their beautiful hellion, and he couldn't wait to notch the play even higher.

Slowly he drew his tongue along her slit, tasting her tangy juices and fighting against the need to consume her whole. He felt as if he'd waited a lifetime for this. His head said he should appreciate the moment while his body demanded entrance and instant gratification.

Allie's hips thrust up toward his mouth as he played with her clit, using his teeth and tongue to drive her to the peak. In just a short time, he'd become addicted to her orgasms, the lovely way she tried for only a moment to hold back before diving headlong into the release. Allie came like she lived. Fast and furious and ready for anything. She was perfect for them. Again the thought that she was really here, letting them touch her, staggered him.

Finally.

Her body was gyrating wildly on the table, responding hotly to Charlie's mouth and fingers on her breasts and his tongue at her clit. He reached up and roughly shoved two fingers into her dripping cunt. She cried out and her climax shook the table with its intensity.

"Shit," he heard Charlie mutter. "Fuck breakfast." His friend leaned down to lift Allie in his arms. "Bedroom," he commanded over his shoulder to Alex.

"I'll be damned if I'm spending one more minute waiting to get inside this sexy body of hers."

Alex grinned and followed them into Charlie's room. Both of them were fairly large men, which led to their purchase of king-sized beds. Placing Allie in the middle on her back, Charlie quickly crawled over her body.

"I need you," he said to her, and Alex wondered at the sound of apology in his friend's voice as he spoke to her.

Allie smiled and enveloped him in her arms, their sweet embrace taking his breath away for a moment. Alex gripped the cherry railing at the foot of Charlie's four-poster bed as Charlie kissed her gently before pulling back to strip away his pants. His motions stirred something in Alex and he crossed to the bedside table, pulling open the drawer. He reached in and grabbed a condom, thrusting it into his friend's hand.

Charlie was positioning himself over Allie and looked up in surprise at Alex's offering.

"Shit. I never forget..." Charlie said, mostly to himself.

"Allie could make a man forget his own name," Alex teased. "Hurry up." As he spoke, he gestured at his own cock, fighting against the constraints of the suddenly too-tight denim.

Charlie grinned and shook his head. "No way in hell am I hurrying up. You'll just have to wait your turn."

"Or," Allie purred from the bed where she'd been quietly watching their exchange, "you could take off those damn jeans and let me have a taste of that. It's clear neither one of you intends to feed me a proper breakfast."

Alex knew she meant her words as a tease, but it only served to enflame them both.

"Oh yeah," he said, quickly stripping off his jeans as Charlie finished putting on the condom. His friend gripped her hips and turned her onto her stomach.

"Hey!" she squealed as Charlie's motions caught her off guard.

"Hands and knees," Charlie demanded gruffly. "I want to watch you suck Alex off while I fuck you from behind."

Allie quickly complied while Alex climbed onto the bed and sat with his back against the headboard. Allie bent down and for the second time took him into her hot mouth. Alex groaned as she accepted his girth more easily this time, swallowing him nearly to the back of her throat on the first pass.

"Fuck," he whispered as Allie paused. Opening his eyes, he found Charlie's gaze on Allie's mouth around his cock.

"I can't tell you how hot that is," Charlie said, their gazes connecting.

Allie squirmed a bit in her own impatience and Alex grinned. "Better take care of our girl. I think she's getting a bit annoyed with waiting for you."

Charlie gripped Allie's hips and placed his cock at the entrance to her body. She tried to push back on him, and Alex watched Charlie's firm hands halt her movements. His friend would control this encounter, and the idea of Charlie's power ratcheted up his own desire. As Charlie pushed into her body, Allie began to suck his cock with such fervent intensity his vision went black. For a moment, Alex was sorry he'd agreed to the blowjob, wishing he could take the time to watch his friends making love. Allie's talented tongue and teasing teeth were certainly distracting him from any chance he had at enjoying the tableau before him.

Charlie's thrusts became stronger, harder, and Alex felt Allie struggling to hold on. He glanced up and sensed Charlie's regret once again as his movements lightened up, slowed a bit.

"I'm sorry," his friend said through gritted teeth. "I'm trying to hold back. Feels too good. I'm too rough but I need this, her—"

Alex reached down and pulled Allie's mouth off his cock. She seemed too mindless with her coming orgasm to realize she'd released him. Glancing up, he saw Charlie tense with the battle to soften his thrusts.

Alex scooted down until his body was lying flat under Allie's. The position left his legs stretched out between Charlie's, but either his friend didn't notice or he simply didn't mind.

Her upper body collapsed on top of him while Charlie still held her hips in his hands. He was thrusting into her but slower now, as if waiting for permission.

"Are you okay, Allie?" Alex whispered, well aware Charlie could hear his question.

"Perfect," she replied quickly, raising her lips to kiss him. She was too enthralled to realize the battle of conscience being waged behind her.

Alex returned her kiss then pulled her head to his chest. "She's perfect," he repeated.

He saw relief cover Charlie's face a split second before the man's body gave up the attempt at holding back. He thrust into her with a force that threw Alex's body into overdrive. Over and over he watched his friend's face, his body, as he made love to Allie—and Alex wondered what it would feel like to be taken with such unrestrained desire and need by him.

He felt Allie come, but Charlie continued to pound into her soft body as if stopping would signal his death. She screamed with her second orgasm, and Alex saw Charlie's body begin to shudder with its own release.

Charlie's beautiful, pained face and Allie's throaty, sexy screams as they climaxed together sent Alex over the edge and he came roughly against Allie's stomach, without a single touch.

Charlie collapsed by his side as Allie lay atop him. His friend's big hand reached over to brush Allie's dark hair out of her face, and Alex felt his heart stop at Charlie's nearness. They were lying naked, side by side, but Charlie didn't seem disturbed by their too-close proximity. It was all Alex could do not to reach over and grasp Charlie's other hand as it lay carelessly next to his.

Allie's soft breathing alerted him to the fact that she'd fallen asleep again.

"We're going to have to do something about this habit she has of passing out every time she has an orgasm," Alex whispered.

Charlie chuckled and spoke in a hushed undertone. "I thought men were supposed to conk out after sex. I'm sorry, man," he added. "I guess you're suffering a serious case of blue balls right about now." Apparently Charlie hadn't noticed Alex's pubescent response to his climax.

"I'm okay. We've got all the time in the world." As soon as the words passed his lips, he saw Charlie's relaxed position stiffen and a cloud of confusion cover his friend's face.

"Do we?" Charlie asked.

Alex sighed, well aware that this conversation was inevitable. Allie shifted slightly on his chest but didn't wake up. He gently lowered her to his opposite side, wondering how Charlie would feel about the two of them lying side by side without Allie as a buffer in the middle. When he didn't move, Alex released a small breath of relief.

"I'm not playing a game, Charlie."

"I didn't think you were. I'm just not sure what it is we're doing here, Alex. I'm in love with Allie. I always have been."

"So have I," Alex challenged. For years he'd suffered in silence over Allie's departure. He was tired of hiding his feelings for the woman. Hell, he was tired of hiding his feelings period.

"Fuck," Charlie said, looking up at the ceiling. "I was afraid of that."

"What's that supposed to mean?"

"Damn, Alex. You're my best friend. I don't want to fight with you over a woman, but Allie…"

"Allie isn't just any woman."

"No, she's not," Charlie said sadly.

"I don't see us fighting over her," Alex added. "I see us sharing her."

Charlie glanced back at him, surprise in the lines of his face. "We can't do this forever."

"Why not?"

His question seemed to stop Charlie in his tracks. "What do you mean, why not? Because this is sex, not a lifestyle, Alex. Shit, I was an ass to have even let this start."

Charlie rose from the bed and reached down to retrieve his pants. As he pulled them up, he walked to the window, never looking back. Alex felt his absence from the bed immediately.

"We can't both keep her," Charlie said after several minutes.

"I'll ask again, why not?"

"Because it's not natural, not normal. Not that I would expect you to understand that. You, who just grabs whatever the hell he wants without considering the consequences," Charlie said.

"What the hell is that supposed to mean?" he asked.

"Dammit, Alex! You don't see the lines, the limits that most normal people see. We can't share Allie forever!" Charlie hissed, obviously struggling not to raise his voice and wake Allie.

"Who says? I can't think of anything more natural than being with you and Allie. We'll move her out of that stupid townhouse and in here with us. We can knock down that damn wall between our houses and renovate the inside. Make it a real home for the three of us."

Charlie reeled back in shock and Alex cursed his wayward tongue. He hadn't meant to throw all his hopes and dreams for the future in his friend's face so soon. Fact was, he'd made sure when they'd built the house that it could easily be remodeled into one. At the time, he'd told Charlie it was just in case they ever had trouble trying to sell it, but in the back of his mind he'd been planning, praying for the day when they'd all move in together.

"Allie's only been home a few weeks. We've spent one night together. It's too soon to make plans like that. Fuck, I think it'll always be too soon for that crazy plan." Charlie's voice was rambling, bewildered.

"I wasn't suggesting we head out to the shed and get the sledgehammers now." Alex was trying to keep his voice light, relaxed. It wouldn't do for Charlie to see how much he was banking on keeping this ménage going. Charlie was clearly still uneasy about them spending the night together.

"Christ, man, I just wasn't expecting it to be this way."

Alex rose from the bed and pulled on his jeans. He crossed the room to stand beside Charlie. "I know it's kind of out there, but I don't think it's completely impossible. There will be some bumps in the road, but we both love her. Before we start making plans for pistols at dawn, let's give this sharing idea a try. If it doesn't work out, we can schedule a fight to the death for her."

Alex's jest had the desired effect, and Charlie laughed for a moment before sobering and looking back toward Allie's sleeping form on the bed.

"I didn't expect the sex to be… I mean, having you in the bed with Allie and me, it's just so…"

Now it was Alex's turn to laugh. Charlie was never at a loss for words. To see him struggling to describe something so indescribable was rather entertaining.

"At least you're finally calling it sex. If you'd tried to call it 'doing the dirty', I think I would have had to punch you in the mouth," Alex teased.

They laughed as Charlie acknowledged the truth in his words. Ever since high school, his friend had jokingly referred to sex as "doing the dirty" and it drove Alex nuts.

Their shared laughter died down slowly and Charlie shook his head. "It will never be that with her," he said at last.

"I know what you mean, man." He reached up and lightly punched Charlie on the arm, thankful that for now, they seemed to have reached a tacit agreement to forge ahead.

"I would like to suggest that the two of us get out there and start rustlin' up some breakfast for that girl. I have a strong suspicion she won't stay with either one of us if we don't start working in some regular mealtimes," Alex joked.

Charlie's laugh was overshadowed by his rumbling stomach. "I'll whip us up some omelets. You can start the coffee." Charlie threw a friendly arm over his shoulders, and Alex felt his heart skip a beat at the motion.

As they walked to the kitchen, Alex couldn't hold back the small sense of relief that he'd narrowly dodged an exploding bomb while trying to work his way out of the damn minefield he'd plopped them all in the midst of.

He also couldn't fight back the feeling that if they made it through safely and with their hearts intact, it would be a miracle.

Chapter Six

Charlie glanced out the front window of his house, certain he'd heard a car on the drive. It had been one week to the day since they'd embarked on this odd love affair, and he still found himself struggling with the idea of it despite the fact the sex was hotter than hell.

Allie had spent last weekend with them before returning to her townhouse on Sunday. Since then, the three of them had gone out for several dinners, getting reacquainted and catching up on the past six years. He had to admit Allie had done some incredible things and seen some amazing places. Hell, half the time he found himself jealous of her experiences. Her face lit up when she talked about the years she'd spent away, and Charlie could see how much she'd grown up, changed.

Typically after dinner, they ended up at one of their houses for some of the hottest, wildest sex he'd ever experienced. Unfortunately Allie hadn't spent an entire night with them since the weekend and Charlie was anxious to change that. He liked the idea of waking up in the morning with her in his arms.

Last night, after they'd dropped her off at her townhouse, she'd promised to come today at five for dinner at his place. It was now seven thirty, and the idea of her walking away, hitting the road and disappearing from their lives again kept playing over and over in his head. He cursed himself for acting like a damn fool. He never behaved this way, never worried about what a woman was or wasn't doing.

Ever since last weekend, he'd felt like a fool, like a teenage boy with his first girlfriend…and boyfriend.

Fuck.

The idea that he was embarking on a new relationship with not just Allie, but Alex as well, was seriously working on his nerves. They'd spent the entire weekend and a good part of this week together in bed, making love, touching, talking, teasing, and everything had felt fresh and new and perfect.

Fuck.

The word perfect seemed to hover in his mind constantly. How could something so innately wrong feel so completely right? The image of Alex kissing Allie, pushing into her with his thick cock and loving her with such tenderness was emblazoned on his brain.

He'd been completely useless at work this week as he constantly felt his thoughts drifting back to their shared time together. Mercifully, Brooks and Travers had both called in sick most of the week. Yeah right. Obviously they hadn't managed to free themselves from the love trap Ginny had set for Travers. For once though, Charlie had been thankful for their absence. He wasn't looking forward to facing Ginny when word of what the two of them had been doing with her sister reached her. Christ, she'd kill them.

Charlie glanced back toward the window, his thoughts of the three of them in bed playing through his mind again. The memories haunted him and left him rock-hard as he found himself mesmerized by the images of Alex as much as Allie. What the hell did that mean?

"You know, a watched pot never boils," came a voice from the doorway dividing his side of the house from Alex's.

"Thanks, Grandma. Any other stupid expressions you wanna lay on me?"

Alex laughed. "How about patience is a virtue? She's running a little late, Charlie. No big deal. Apparently, time has not made your heart grow fonder because if it had, you would remember that Allie is one of those people who always plans to be somewhere on time but never is. Twenty bucks says she walks in here with some epic tale about why she's so late."

"You're on," Charlie said, praying he'd have to fork over the money. He just couldn't shake the idea that they'd come on too strong and Allie had split to escape them.

Tires on the driveway put him out of his misery. “Ah,” Alex said as the headlights of Allie’s car flashed through the window. “Right on time.”

Three minutes later, Allie crashed through the front door of Charlie’s side of the house, her arms laden with packages and catalogs and a large duffel bag slung over her shoulder.

“Oh my God,” Allie said breathlessly. “You would not believe the day I’ve had.”

Alex flashed a grin over his shoulder at him, and Charlie struggled not to roll his eyes. The moment the words left her mouth, the past came crashing around him and he suddenly recalled Allie saying those exact same words about a thousand times in their youth. He grinned and fought hard against the laughter bubbling in his chest. He didn’t want Allie to think he was laughing at her as she began to recite a tale of woe longer and more action-packed than Homer’s Odyssey. As she continued to talk, he reached into his back pocket and retrieved his wallet. Taking out a crisp new twenty, he handed it to Alex.

“What was that for?” Allie asked, taking a break in her story.

“Just remembered I owed Alex some money,” he answered vaguely. “Go on with your story. What happened after the plumber left?”

Allie started talking again, and Charlie could see Alex was enjoying the sweet sound of her voice as much as he was. The woman knew how to tell a damn funny story, relying heavily on hyperbole to really pack a punch.

"So it's official," she said. "I'm a student again."

"Interior decorating, huh?" Alex mused, and Charlie was grateful his friend had been paying attention. He'd been so distracted by her pink lip gloss and wondering how it would taste, he'd obviously missed a few details in her list of the day's events.

"I figured why not?" Allie replied. "I mean, Jim left me a hell of a lot of money, but I'm only twenty-eight years old. I don't wanna spend my days prancing around like Paris fucking Hilton. I'd be bored after ten minutes. So I'm going to take a few classes and try to get a job doing something I enjoy."

"You'd be good at interior design," Charlie added, looking around his living room. During the course of the week, she'd moved all the furniture and hung up a few pictures. He couldn't believe the difference it made. "I'm glad you had a productive day, Allie, but I think maybe we should have a little discussion about cell phones and what they're used for."

"Cell phones?" she asked.

"You're two and half hours late. Did it never occur to you to give us a call or text?" He was too relieved by her arrival to really be angry, and he wondered for a moment how long it would take him to get over the constant fear that she could leave at any minute.

"Oh well, yeah, I did think about it, but I forgot to charge it. I mean, between trying to register for classes and with the lack of water at the townhouse, I just didn't think about it."

"No worries, hellion," Alex said, wrapping his arms around her waist from behind and placing his chin on her shoulder. Charlie sucked in a breath, awestruck by how good they looked together, how right. "You're here now and that's all that matters. I hope the size of that duffel means you packed enough stuff to stay awhile. More than just tonight, maybe?"

"I can't exactly stay in a townhouse with no water. I was sort of hoping I could shack up here with you guys 'til it's fixed. If that's a problem, I'm sure Ginny would let me—"

"You're staying here," Charlie interrupted, picking up her duffel bag and leading the way back to his bedroom. "Indefinitely," he added gruffly, annoyed that she thought she even had to ask and definitely not caring if the plumber ever got the water running.

Allie giggled. "Oh my, someone sounds grumpy."

"Charlie's not exactly the most patient man. He was worried about you, hellion."

"I wasn't worried. I was merely concerned."

Allie and Alex laughed at his comment and he couldn't help but join in.

"If you two are finished having fun at my expense, I've got dinner ready to go. We'll be lucky if the lasagna isn't dry as hell at this point."

* * *

After dinner, they watched a movie on the flat screen in Alex's living room. Charlie grinned, looking down at his friends sprawled out on the oversized sectional couch. Allie's head was resting on his lap while his feet were propped up on a soft ottoman. Alex was stretched out on one elbow and spooning Allie from behind, his head just barely grazing Charlie's shoulder.

"You sure do know how to live in comfort," Allie teased, and Charlie was surprised to find her thoughts mirroring his so closely. "Amazing shower, super-sized TV and bed, the softest couch on the planet."

"What can I say? I've been a bachelor for too long. Too much money and not enough practical stuff to spend it on. Besides, I like to be comfortable," Alex replied.

Allie giggled. "And what do you consider practical stuff, if not furniture?"

"I should be spending all my money on spoiling a wife."

Charlie glanced over at his friend to see if he was joking. Never in all their years of friendship had Alex ever mentioned marriage. Allie seemed discomfited by his comment as well, and Charlie wondered where she thought this cozy little triangle of theirs was headed.

She surprised him by responding matter-of-factly. "I've never really pictured myself getting married."

"What?" Alex asked. "You gotta be kidding me. You'd be an amazing wife."

Allie laughed at his words. "Oh my God, shut up, Alex. I would suck at it and you know it. I mean look at me, I can't even date normally."

Charlie's blood chilled at her words. "Allie, if this is bothering you... If you're uncomfortable with the three of us—"

"Oh no, Charlie." She sat up quickly and placed a finger against his lips. "That's the problem. I love being here with the two of you. I think maybe I love it a little bit too much."

"What's the problem with that?" Alex asked.

"I don't see myself ever wanting this to end."

Charlie sighed a breath of relief before realizing her words shouldn't be so comforting to him.

"Jesus, you and Charlie sure are birds of a feather," Alex said, pulling Allie back down in front of him.

"What's that supposed to mean?" Allie asked.

"Again with the granny lines," Charlie said at the same time.

"It means you're both so worried about what you think can't be that you're losing sight of what could be."

Alex's words resonated deep within Charlie and he could feel the truth behind them. Allie's hand tightened on his knee and Charlie placed his hand atop hers.

She looked toward the television, but when she spoke, Charlie knew her thoughts weren't on the movie. "I can see us lying here like this twenty years from now," she confessed.

Charlie saw Alex grin at her admission. "So can I," his friend added.

Leaning back and gazing unseeingly at the TV, Charlie felt their words in his heart. "So can I," he whispered.

Allie sat up again and turned to face them before leaning down and placing a long, hot kiss on Alex's lips. Charlie reached over and ran his fingers through her hair, entranced by the depths of her passion. She released Alex and turned toward him, giving him the same enthusiastic embrace. Charlie felt Alex move closer—and he was overcome by the feeling that he wanted to kiss both of them.

The impact of his thoughts jarred him. Allie, perhaps sensing his confusion, pulled back to look at him.

"Kiss him," she whispered almost soundlessly.

Charlie remained motionless. How could she have known? He turned his head, surprised by the look of unbridled yearning in Alex's eyes.

But rather than looking at Allie, his friend was looking at him.

Shoving his rampant thoughts aside, Charlie decided to move on instinct and leaned in. Alex shadowed his move and before he knew what was happening, they were kissing.

Charlie had never imagined what it would be like to kiss another man. Shit, the idea would have seemed completely foreign to him before this past oh-too-wild week. Suddenly all the walls that had been constructed around his limited view of the world began to crumble as he felt Alex's hand in his hair, pulling him deeper into the kiss, holding him captive to the feeling of his lips and tongue and teeth.

Allie's soft breath touched his cheek only seconds before her lips, and Charlie turned toward her, taking her mouth again. The three of them nestled together, taking turns kissing, and time seemed to have stopped completely as they were enveloped by the perfect unity of the moment.

"Bedroom," Charlie muttered when he felt as if he'd explode from the sensations and need.

"Yes," Alex hissed, and the three of them stumbled down the hall together, touching, kissing, undressing each other, afraid to break the connection of their lips and bodies.

They were all naked by the time they hit the bedroom, and Allie hopped onto the bed, beckoning them with her finger and a seductive smile.

Alex grinned and crawled up beside her, but Charlie hung back for a moment, trying to halt the uncultivated emotions crashing down on him.

"Uh-oh," Allie said between giggles as Alex tickled her bare midriff. "Charlie's thinking again."

He shook his head at her teasing words and shook off the heavy weight that threatened to crush him. For tonight, for this moment, he'd take a page from their book and live in the now. There would be plenty of time later to consider the repercussions. Right now he wanted to be with them.

Joining them on the bed, he pulled Allie toward him, taking her lips in a hard kiss. He mentally chastised himself for his roughness and pulled back a bit. He felt as if he had to constantly be on guard with her. She was so much smaller than him, so delicate. He'd rather cut off his arm than hurt her, but he couldn't resist the need driving him to take her hard and fast.

"Easy," he heard Alex mutter when his hands started laying claim to Allie's gorgeous, soft curves. Charlie couldn't seem to touch her fast enough, cover sufficient ground quickly enough. There was a raging inferno building inside him, scorching everything in its path.

"We have all night," Alex said, wrapping his hand around one of Charlie's wrists.

Charlie felt the heat in his friend's gesture, but rather than calm him as he was sure Alex intended, it stoked the flames higher. He shook off Alex's grip and pulled his friend's face closer, resuming the forbidden kisses they'd begun on the couch. His lips trailed along Alex's jaw as Allie's hands traveled along his chest, toying with his nipples.

If this was what it felt like to be insane, Charlie was ready and willing to have himself committed for life.

A low moan came from Alex, and the deep, wholly masculine sound of it pulled Charlie from his trancelike state.

He was making out with his best friend.

He mentally shook off the panic building inside him as Allie's soft lips landed on his chest, dragging her tongue along his rib cage. Turning away from Alex, he pushed Allie back on the bed, determined to push away the unease he felt when he looked at his friend.

This is wrong.

The words crashed around his head, and he couldn't seem to shake them from his rattled brain and shredded wits.

"Together," he heard Allie whisper, and he only had a second to wonder at her words when she took him by surprise, pushing him to his back. It was a testament to his confusion that he let her take the lead. He never gave a woman control in the bedroom. He'd never allowed another to guide his sexual play but, as Allie's breasts rubbed against his chest, he felt the reins slip from his grasp and he didn't bother to try to pick them up again.

He took her hips in his hands and pulled her down on top of him, relishing the feeling of her body as his cock entered her and she started to ride him, slowly, luxuriously. He heard Alex reaching for something in the nightstand, but his eyes were closed, too focused, too intent on the pleasure Allie was provoking inside him. She was a miracle, a gift he'd never had the nerve to wish for. He loved her with his whole heart.

The bed shifted by his thighs and Allie's motions stilled.

He forced himself to open his eyes, forced himself to look over her shoulder at the man behind her. For a split second he'd allowed himself to forget Alex was there, but he now watched the gentle way Alex pushed Allie forward so that her body lay prostrate atop his. As he watched his friend work lubrication into Allie's ass, he felt the walls closing in yet again.

Although the three of them had been together numerous times the past several days, they'd always taken turns and neither man had breached Allie's ass. She had confided that although she'd participated in anal play before, it was nothing more than a finger. Now Charlie felt spellbound by the image of Alex's face as he worked his fingers into her virgin bud. Allie squirmed slightly and Charlie engulfed her in his embrace.

"Shhh," he soothed, running a hand through her long hair. "You are amazing," he whispered, and he saw Alex smile at his words.

Once Alex had worked three fingers in, he reached down and retrieved a condom he must have pulled out of the drawer with the lube. As he watched Alex tear the package open with his teeth and don it, he realized he'd forgotten to do the same.

"Allie," he whispered. "Are you on the Pill?"

"Yes," she muttered against his chest, and he felt a small sense of relief.

His question must have drawn Alex's attention to the oversight, and he wondered what his friend would say. Would he be angry at him? He watched his friend shrug and grin before resuming on his intended path. Alex pressed the head of his cock into Allie's tight ass, and Charlie swallowed heavily, amazed to realize he could feel so much. Every move his friend made in Allie's body touched him.

Slowly Alex penetrated her ass, and it wasn't until he was fully seated that Charlie felt Allie expel her held breath. Charlie sighed as well and realized he hadn't been breathing throughout Alex's entrance either.

The thick hardness of Alex's cock rubbed against his own through the thin membrane inside Allie, and Charlie couldn't contain the moan of ecstasy that escaped his lips.

Alex caught his gaze and he knew his friend was silently asking for permission to move. The sexual tension in the room was thicker than fog, and Charlie wished he could stay lost in the haze forever. With a single, slight nod, he watched as Alex began his retreat, and Charlie sucked in a breath as his friend's cock traveled down the length of his own, rubbing and caressing it in a way so foreign yet so glorious. How had he lived without this?

He looked down, almost afraid of the expression he would find on Allie's face. Was this too much for her? Was it too painful? Too overwhelming? Too soon?

She lifted her head from his chest and kissed him gently. "I've never felt so…" She paused and Charlie knew she was struggling with the same powerful emotions as he.

"Me, either," he whispered, kissing her again as he and Alex started to move within her in tandem. Charlie knew none of them would last long. It didn't seem to matter how many times they came into her body, neither he nor Alex could withstand the need to come quickly. He chuckled at the thought, aware that they would need to work on that small problem or risk destroying Allie's opinion of their sexual prowess.

"What's so funny?" Allie asked, gasping as Alex thrust into her once more with more power than before.

Charlie groaned at the impact, stars beginning to form behind his eyes. "I can't seem to last more than five minutes with you."

Alex moaned above him, apparently finding Charlie's confession comforting. "Thank God," his friend muttered. "I was afraid I was about to seriously embarrass myself. I can't—"

The rest of Alex's words were lost in his orgasm and his throbbing, pulsing cock triggered Charlie's climax.

"Fuck!" he gritted out, overwhelmed by the feeling of coming inside a woman's body without a condom. The feeling was frighteningly addictive and Charlie feared he'd never want to wear one with her again.

Allie cried out as Charlie became aware of Alex's finger toying with her clit. He cursed his selfishness, grateful his friend was cognizant enough to see to Allie's pleasure. She trembled and her inner muscles gripped his cock so tightly, he felt himself begin to harden almost instantly.

Allie and Alex must have felt it as well.

"Oh no," Allie said, breathlessly. "You guys are going to be the death of me."

"I believe Charlie pointed out that we all came a bit quick that time. I feel certain with a little practice we could really perfect our sustaining time," Alex joked.

Allie giggled quietly before resting her head on Charlie's chest. For several moments none of them moved, the sensations, the connection too new, too precious to break. Before long, Allie's breathing deepened and Charlie shook his head, realizing she'd fallen asleep yet again. They were all still intimately hooked together. Glancing at his friend, he watched Alex flash him a football signal from their high school days, and in unison they shifted. Charlie rolled onto his left side, gently keeping Allie tucked against his chest, while Alex followed the move and remained resolutely spooned to her back.

Alex's low laugh drifted over to him and he raised his hand above Allie's shoulder. Charlie grinned at the gesture. They'd been hell on the gridiron with that left fake, and without a thought, Charlie quietly high-fived him and joined in his laughter.

"She'd have kicked our asses if she'd seen that," Alex whispered. "Probably think we were gloating or something. Never thought that move would come in so handy..." Alex snuggled into the pillow and Charlie heard his friend's light breathing. Damn man could fall asleep in seconds.

Charlie rested his hand on Allie's waist and wished he could find sleep as well. Instead he was aching with the heaviness in his chest that told him this happiness couldn't, shouldn't last.

Chapter Seven

"Where's Charlie?" Allie asked, walking into the kitchen and thanking God for the full pot of coffee awaiting her.

"Where do you think?" Alex asked, and Allie winced at his hurt, angry tone. Since their super-sexy mating last Friday, Charlie had gone into virtual hiding. Although they'd spent most of the weekend in bed, she'd sensed his mental retreat. He never kissed Alex again, and he refused to repeat the double penetration that had left Allie so breathless, so captivated. He'd claimed he didn't want to hurt her by doing it again so soon.

Once the weekend ended, Charlie started heading into work early every morning and returning home very late at night. He hadn't joined them in the bedroom again, instead sleeping in his own bed rather than joining them in Alex's.

When Allie had tried to confront him about it, he'd brushed her concerns aside, insisting that he was working on a big project and claiming he'd not wanted to wake them up when they were sleeping so peacefully. She could feel the distance he was trying to put between them, but she wasn't sure what to say to pull him back. It was clear he was upset, thinking they'd crossed a line they shouldn't have.

Alex refused to approach Charlie at all, and Allie sensed for the first time that her confident lover was truly at a loss about what to do. She'd grown so accustomed to him merely grabbing the bull by the horns and accepting nothing less than what he wanted that it was frightening to see him so uncertain, so apprehensive and insecure. Needless to say, it had been the longest week of her life.

"Man, am I glad it's Friday," she said lightly, feigning a carefree attitude. "What do you want to do this weekend?"

She watched Alex grab a cold bagel from the bag on the counter. He'd been trying to put on a good face for her this week, but she knew his attempts at remaining positive were wearing him out. They'd both thought that Charlie had only needed a bit of time to adjust, to come to grips with what happened. He lifted the hard bread to his lips and she gripped his wrist.

"Why don't you let me cut that and toast it? Wouldn't you like it a bit more with cream cheese or butter?" she asked.

He shrugged. "It's fine like this."

"Alex, I think maybe you should talk to Charlie. It's clear this silent treatment you guys are maintaining isn't working." Alex had adamantly insisted two nights ago that a confrontation wouldn't change things, and Allie had hesitantly abided by his wishes. She realized that she couldn't help Charlie, only Alex could—and that wouldn't happen as long as they were avoiding each other.

"You're with him all day," she said. "Just go in his office and have it out. Stop letting him hide from this…from us."

"Dammit, Allie! He's not hiding. He doesn't want it, okay? I told you six years ago. He's not fucking gay. It's pretty damn clear he hated what happened last weekend and now he doesn't want to see me."

"I don't think it's clear he hated anything," Allie retorted, her own temper wearing thin under the stressful living conditions. "Is that what you think?"

"He was repulsed by what happened, Allie. What we did. He's probably sickened by it."

"Holy shit. You've lost your mind too! Is that what you've been thinking this whole week? That Charlie didn't like kissing you, touching you? Talk about somebody being blind."

"Why else would he be avoiding me? Avoiding us?" Alex walked to the kitchen table and sat down heavily. "I owe you an apology for that," he said softly.

"For what?"

"Charlie would still be here, still be with you if I hadn't forced myself on him. Hadn't forced myself into your relationship."

Allie's rage broke free and she picked up a bagel and threw it at him, hard.

"Ow!" he cried as the bread bounced off his forehead and hit a wall. "What the hell did you do that for?"

"I'm hoping to knock some damn sense into you! Tell you what, why don't I go over a few things for the idiots in the peanut gallery here."

Alex looked around and gave her an amused grin. "I'm the only person in the room," he said.

"Like I said, idiot." Her anger was still full force and showing no signs of abating despite Alex's guilty, apologetic looks.

"Number one, we are a trio—not a couple plus one, but a bona fide threesome. There is no 'Charlie and me' without you, so go ahead and get that thought out of your head. Number two, Charlie was not repulsed by what happened between the two of you. I was there, and apparently the only person in the bedroom paying attention. If Charlie is avoiding us, it's because he loved every single minute of our fucking and it freaked him out. He's not like you and me—a fact we have a tendency to forget every now and then. Charlie lives in a world where one man and one woman spend a lifetime together monogamously. He sincerely believes in relationships where he protects and cherishes a woman while leading the sexual play in the bedroom."

Alex nodded and started to respond, but Allie cut him off with her hand.

"I'm not finished," she said. "In the course of two weeks, we've asked him to participate in a ménage, give up some of his control in the bedroom and thrust him into a physical relationship with you, his best friend and a man. Talk about culture shock."

"It all happened too fast," Alex interjected, and Allie waved him off again, picking up another bagel. Alex threw his hands up in time and knocked the bread away before it hit her desired target. "Dammit, Allie, stop throwing shit at me!"

"In what world is six years too fast, Einstein? Hell, it's been longer than that, even. When did you first realize you were in love with Charlie?"

Alex shrugged. "A lifetime ago," he answered sadly.

"So if anything, you've almost waited too long."

He nodded, and his shoulders lowered dejectedly. "You're probably right. It's too late now."

"Holy hell, you are dense! I said almost too long. For someone who knows what they want, you sure as hell don't know how to go after it."

Alex rose from the table, his frustration pouring off him in waves. “Face it. I’m asking for too much, Allie. I want more than Charlie can give.”

“I don’t hear you asking for a damn thing. You keep plotting all these sneak attacks rather than confronting him with the truth. Go talk to him. Tell him how you feel. Stop hiding.”

Alex shook his head, but she could see him considering her words. “If he left—”

“He won’t leave,” she whispered, secretly praying her words were true.

“You did,” he answered, and his two softly spoken words took her breath away.

All these years he’d thought he’d run her off, scared her away. She had thought she’d convinced him of the error of this thinking, but obviously the residual pain was still lingering.

“I’m so sorry,” she said, walking over and wrapping her hands around his waist. “I’m so very, very sorry. Here I am yelling at you for hiding your feelings when all along I’ve done the same damn thing.”

Alex embraced her with his strong arms and she relished the power in them. He was tall, like Charlie, but bulkier, built like a bodybuilder, and she continually marveled at the fact he could make her five-foot-six frame feel tiny.

"Sounds like we've all made a few mistakes along the way," Alex said, his chin resting on the top of her head. "Probably to be expected, considering what we're attempting to achieve."

She pulled back to look up at him and offered the words she'd yet to speak to either man. It was time they all came out of hiding. "I love you, Alex. So very, very much."

He grinned, leaning down to brush a light kiss against her lips. "I love you too, hellion."

"Go talk to Charlie," she insisted. "Tell him how you feel."

"If he leaves—" he started, but she covered his lips quickly with her fingers.

"I'll still be here."

* * *

"So we kissed, Charlie," Alex said as he walked into his best friend's office, slamming the door behind him. Brooks and Travers had stepped out for a long lunch, and Alex had decided Allie was right. Enough was enough. Charlie had shut him down for days and he couldn't take the distance, the silence, any longer. He knew his best friend was struggling with what that kiss and the heated interlude that followed meant, but Alex couldn't stand being ignored, treated like a leper.

"If you can't handle that, then fine. Throw a punch at me, key my car, move out, trash my office, yell…something! I don't give a fuck what you do, but stop shutting me out. Things got a little intense the other night. I know that, but this silent treatment is just pissing me off."

Charlie stood, and Alex wondered for a moment if his friend was going to take him up on the punch. He certainly looked angry enough to kick some serious ass.

"Why aren't you freaked out?" Charlie asked hotly, and Alex stumbled back a step at his question.

"What?"

"You were there too, Alex. You were touching and kissing me back. Why is it I seem to be the only one struggling with that fact?"

Shit. Alex had been ready for the anger, but now that he was faced with actually confessing how he'd felt from the start, he became tongue-tied. He'd hidden his feelings for years and, despite Allie's assurance that things would work out, Alex couldn't kick free from the one question that haunted him. What if Charlie left? He didn't think he could survive if Charlie left him.

"I…I'm struggling," he said, though the words sounded exactly like the big fucking lie they were.

"No," Charlie said, walking closer to him. "I don't think you are, Alex. In fact, I think somewhere deep inside that conniving mind of yours you plotted for this to happen all along."

"Conniving mind?" Alex repeated angrily, Allie's similar comment in the kitchen this morning floated through his mind. What had she called it? His sneak attack?

The pressure of restraining his emotions for so many years broke free in a whirlwind of irrational, uncontainable rage. “Is that what I’m doing, Charlie? Plotting to put you and Allie into an uncomfortable situation? Forcing the two of you into a ménage as some sort of game? Is that what you think? Why? Why would I do that? To fuck with your minds? To get my jollies? You think it’s fun for me to have my heart ripped out at every turn just because I made the fucked-up mistake of falling in love with both of you? Go to hell, Anderson! I’m sick of this shit! I’m gettin’ outta here.” Alex turned to leave, anger and heartbreak roaring through his system.

“Oh no you’re not!” Charlie gripped his upper arm, pulling him around roughly.

Alex, his nerves shattered, turned with his fists clenched and ready. Before he could swing, Charlie shoved him back against the closed office door, leaned in and took his lips in a brutal kiss.

Alex was too shocked to respond, but Charlie didn’t seem to notice. Charlie claimed his mouth with the same unbridled passion he’s seen him offer to Allie.

Alex pulled away. “Don’t. Not if you don’t want what comes with this. I won’t be shut out again.”

Charlie reached up and gripped his face between his hands. Their faces were so close, their breathing so hot and heavy, Alex felt consumed, burned by it.

"I want it," Charlie barked out. When his lips touched Alex's this time, Alex was ready. He twisted his hands in Charlie's shirt, pulling him closer, dragging their erections against each other through the material of their pants. Alex wanted there to be no misunderstanding about where he hoped this would lead. The fear of that misapprehension fled when Charlie lowered one hand to Alex's ass and pulled him even closer.

The temperature in the office shot up and Alex suddenly couldn't stand the unbearable scratchiness of the clothing on his body. He ripped the buttons from their slots on Charlie's dress shirt. Buttons bounced off the wall and floor, but Charlie paid no mind. He reached for the belt of Alex's trousers, tugging it loose, ripping it free. He dropped it to the floor and immediately went for the button and zipper of his pants.

"Take them off," Charlie commanded as he pushed Alex's pants and boxers down over his hips. Alex toed off his shoes, kicking the infernal material free. Their lips never stopped exploring throughout their disrobing. Alex bent down to take one of Charlie's nipples between his teeth. The excited hiss that flew from his friend's mouth encouraged him to move his torment to the other. Charlie's hands were rough in his hair, directing his movements, holding him to his chest for several moments before pulling his face back to his for another kiss.

Charlie was directing their play, but Alex didn't give a shit. He was here in his best friend's arms, and he was living the dream he'd feared would never come true.

"Desk," Charlie said, grabbing Alex's arm and directing him across the room. Alex heard Charlie loosening the fastening of his own pants. "Lean over. Put your hands flat on the surface."

Alex obeyed, waiting with unconcealed anticipation. He watched as Charlie rounded the desk and pulled a bag from the bottom drawer.

"I bought this stuff last week for us to use with Allie. Forgot about it until now. I didn't think…" His words drifted away and Alex saw him pull out a few sex toys, a new tube of lubrication and a jumbo box of condoms. He watched as his friend pulled on the latex shield then slathered it with a generous amount of the slippery gel. He thought he sensed a moment's hesitation in Charlie's movements, but then his friend looked at him and the uncertainty disappeared.

"Fuck me," Alex whispered.

Charlie shook his head as if in disbelief then grinned. "I won't go easy on you," he said, the familiar lilt of teasing in his voice.

"I didn't expect you would."

Finished with words, Charlie placed the tube of lubrication against the pucker of his ass, working in some of the slippery gel with two fingers. Over and over he worked to loosen the tight opening, and Alex struggled to breathe against the powerful sensations his fingers roused. Satisfied with his work, Charlie replaced his fingers with the head of his cock before pausing again. "You've done this before."

His question came out as a statement, but Alex decided to give his friend the truth.

"Yes," he replied.

Charlie digested his answer for only a second—then slowly slid into him, one exhilarating, glorious inch at a time until he was seated to the hilt.

Alex grunted, fighting not to roar his triumph as Charlie retreated and returned, each thrust gaining speed, momentum. For someone new to homoerotic sex, Charlie seemed to know exactly what to do. Each stroke touched his prostate, rubbing against the oh-so-sensitive nerve endings, and Alex feared that after all his years of waiting he'd embarrass himself in an instant.

"Fuck," he gritted out, pushing back, silently begging for more of Charlie's rough loving.

"God damn, you feel good! I can't, I won't…" One of Charlie's hands ventured around and gripped Alex's erection. "I'm not coming alone," he added, working his fist against the turgid flesh.

"Jesus, man! You're killing me," Alex panted, fighting against his imminent orgasm. His balls tightened and he knew he wouldn't make it much longer.

"Oh God," Charlie said, thrusting harder, faster, working Alex's cock with the same vigor he was using to pound inside his ass. "Now!" he demanded, and Alex gave himself up to the climax, semen shooting from the end of his cock in great spurts that he watched slide down the side of Charlie's desk.

Above him, he could hear Charlie's own cries of release, and he felt the pulsing of his thick cock as he came inside him.

For several moments neither of them moved. Charlie, still lodged within him, held him caged tightly against the desk as both of them gasped for breath.

Finally Charlie stood, pulling free, and Alex instantly missed the fullness, the closeness.

He heard Charlie pull up his pants, heard the rasping sound of the zipper. He forced himself upright, his shirt falling to cover his now-soft cock. For a second he struggled to turn around, to face Charlie after the fact. What was his friend feeling? Remorse, regret, relief?

Turning slowly, he looked behind him, surprised to see Charlie grinning at him a bit self-consciously.

"Okay?" Alex asked, his voice rough, tight.

"Yeah," he answered a bit breathlessly. "But somebody's gonna have to clean off that desk."

Alex laughed and shook his head. "Sorry, buddy. I'm just the kitchen help. It's your desk."

Charlie chuckled and nodded, but his grin faded quickly. "Allie," he said softly.

Alex was confused by his response. "What about her?"

"She won't understand this. I never meant to hurt her, to cheat on her."

Alex reared back at Charlie's words. "Cheat on her? Jesus, Charlie, what the hell are you talking about? This wasn't cheating."

Charlie turned away from him and walked toward the couch in his office, sinking down slowly, heavily, as if weighted down by the pressure of the world on his shoulders.

"She'll understand. Hell, if I know that woman, the only thing she'll be pissed about is that we didn't wait for her," Alex said, crossing the room and sitting down beside his friend, his lover. He reached over and pulled Charlie to him, overwhelmed by the constant need to kiss his friend, touch him. He wondered if that need would ever abate.

As their lips parted, they leaned forward, resting their foreheads together, breathing in each other's air and basking in their newfound closeness.

"I hope you're right," Charlie said.

Alex laughed softly. "I'm always right," he teased. "I've known for years how good it would be between all of us."

Charlie pulled back and looked at him. "Years?"

Alex silently chastised himself. He was feeling so giddy, so relieved, that he found everything he'd been holding back for a lifetime come bubbling to the top. "I've always wanted you."

Charlie shook his head. "Shit, Alex. I keep sitting here waiting for the strangeness to creep in. Waiting for the 'what the fuck have I done' feeling to sink in. It's not coming."

Reaching down, Alex grasped Charlie's hand. "I hope to God it never comes."

Charlie leaned his head back against the couch, squeezing Alex's hand in his as he closed his eyes. "Christ. Me too. Fact of the matter is I'm already thinking I'd really like to do that again."

Alex laughed at his friend's admission, but before they could say more, the bell that hung over the front door rang in the foyer and he glanced at his watch. "Crap. My one thirty meeting is early. I have to go."

"Yeah, you do," Charlie said, looking up at him. His smile didn't quite reach his blue eyes.

"We'll talk when we get home. We'll talk to Allie. Everything will be fine, Charlie. I swear."

Charlie nodded, but Alex couldn't kick the feeling that his friend didn't believe a word he'd just said.

Charlie watched Alex redress before slipping out of his office. He sat still for several moments, trying to figure out what the hell had just happened.

He'd taken his best friend across the top of his desk. He'd had sex with another man. Never in his wildest dreams would he have imagined succumbing to such a thing, but now that it had happened he couldn't find it in himself to regret it. He couldn't believe how much he'd enjoyed it, enjoyed being inside Alex, not having to worry about hurting him, about being too rough.

He'd always been a forceful lover. It was one of the reasons why he'd invested in the Way Down Under Club. He could find willing partners who didn't mind the fact that he liked his sex with an edge of pain. He'd been terrified ever since taking Allie to his bed that he'd hurt her. Every time he'd entered her, he'd fought back the instinct that begged to be set free, that demanded he take her hard and fast, just as he'd done with Alex.

He ran his hand through his hair and sighed. Jesus, in two weeks he'd run the gamut of emotions. He was so damn tired of thinking, he couldn't focus on anything other than the desire to crawl into a bed and sleep for a month.

Allie, the woman of his dreams, had returned home, and he'd pulled her into a ménage with his best friend rather than working toward the happily ever after he'd always imagined for them. Now he couldn't even think of planning a future with her without Alex.

And Alex. Holy hell, the man had gotten under his skin in ways Charlie had never allowed himself to consider before, and now he couldn't see a way back to the platonic friendship he'd always relied on. Worse, he didn't want to find a way back.

Worst of all, he couldn't seem to find a way back to himself, to the things he'd always known and understood to be true about the world. He was a dominant, heterosexual man with a jealous streak a mile wide. He didn't share lovers. He didn't sleep with men. He didn't lose control in the bedroom.

Where the hell had that man gone? In the course of two weeks he'd shared the love of his life with his best friend and then turned around and made love with the man. Regardless of Alex's assurances, Charlie couldn't shake the feeling that he, that they had betrayed Allie.

He'd screwed up royally…with both of them.

Now what am I supposed to do?

Chapter Eight

"Hey, hellion. I'm home," Alex said as Allie greeted him at the front door. She wrapped her arms around his neck and pulled him into a warm, wet kiss. "Damn, I could get used to coming home like this."

Allie looked at him suspiciously as they parted. "You're in an unusually good mood."

He laughed. "Yeah, well, I got smart today and listened to my girlfriend's good advice."

"You talked to Charlie?" she asked.

Alex nodded. "Yep."

She smacked him on the arm and gave him a frustrated growl. "Well, hurry up and spill, then. Don't make me pull all the details out of you. What happened?"

"Charlie didn't say anything?" he asked, glancing over her shoulder. "Where is he? Taking a shower or something?"

"He's not here. He never came home. I was starting to worry because you were both so late."

"He's not here?" Alex repeated, clearly surprised by that fact.

"No, he's not. Should he be?"

"He left the office three hours ago. I had a couple of meetings this afternoon and the last one ran long." Alex pulled out his cell as he spoke, and Allie could see the concern in his face as he dialed Charlie's number. "Shit. It's going straight to voicemail."

There was an urgency, an underlying panic in Alex's voice.

"What happened at work today?" she asked, her heart racing with sudden fear.

"I did what you said. I went into his office and confronted him," Alex said, starting to pace across the living room.

Allie watched his nervous movements and took a deep breath. "What happened?" she repeated. "What did you say?"

"I told him to hit me."

Allie felt a brief spurt of laughter erupt at Alex's words and she rolled her eyes. "Typical male suggestion. Why talk about emotions when you can fight? You've got a small bruise on your forehead, but I suspect that's from the bagel. Since I don't see any other visible wounds, I assume he didn't take you up on your offer."

"No, but we did argue and then…"

“And then?” she prodded.

“We had sex.”

Whatever Allie had been expecting to hear, those three words were not it. “You had sex? With each other?”

“No, Allie, with the cleaning lady,” Alex replied hotly. “Yes with each other!”

“Well…that’s great!” She smiled, pleased that things finally seemed to be falling into place.

“Yeah, great,” Alex agreed.

“That’s better than great. It’s terrific! How was it?”

Alex laughed and shook his head at her. She was one in a million and he thanked God for her every day. “It was earth-shattering. Awesome. There aren’t words to describe it. He wanted to be there, Allie. He wanted me. I never thought…”

Allie put her hands on her hips and feigned anger at Alex’s narrative. “I can’t believe you guys didn’t wait for me,” she joked.

“I told Charlie you’d be pissed about that, but…” Again Alex paused and Allie suddenly recalled Charlie’s MIA status.

“But?”

“He seemed to think you would be upset.”

“Well, I am upset, but probably not in the way Charlie meant,” she said. “What can I say? I’m selfish. I don’t like the idea of being left out of the fun, but I think maybe it was better that the two of you were alone together this first time. Maybe it took some of the pressure off him—wondering and worrying about my response."

"I don't know if you're right about that. Charlie seemed to view what we did as us cheating on you."

Allie was astonished by Alex's words. "What? Is he insane? Where the hell would he get that idea?"

Alex laughed. "That's what I said, but I think this sort of falls under the category you mentioned before. Charlie's ideas of the world are different from ours. He tends to get hung up on so-called normal things."

Allie bit her lower lip and pondered his words, fighting back her own laughter. "You know what the problem is?"

"What?" he asked.

"Nice, ordinary Charlie has been sucked into Allie and Alex Land, where anything goes. I think it's safe to assume we've rocked his foundation quite soundly."

"Shit, I'd say we've crushed his foundation to dust. What the hell are we going to do, Allie? What if he's taken off for good?"

"He hasn't," Allie replied, unsure why she was so certain of that fact. "For one thing, Charlie is as reliable as the tide. He wouldn't just take off from the firm without a word. He's also pretty predictable in a male sort of way."

"What's that supposed to mean?" Alex asked.

"If he thinks he's been unfaithful to me, he's probably hit a local bar and is drinking a bit of liquid courage in order to confess."

"The Way Down Under Club."

"What?" Allie asked.

"He'll be at the club. We have our own rooms there and I'll bet you anything—"

"Wait a minute. You have your own rooms? At a sex club?"

Alex grinned guiltily. "Did I forget to mention we're part owners?"

Allie narrowed her eyes. "Yeah, I think you did."

"He'll be at the club," Alex repeated, and Allie had to agree.

She turned quickly, walking back toward Alex's bedroom.

"Where are you going?" he called out.

"If we're going to a sex club, I have to change my clothes. Hee-hee," she teasingly giggled. "I'm finally getting back in that joint. Give me fifteen minutes."

* * *

Charlie sat in a corner of the bar at the Way Down Under Club and tried to forget the fact that he was sitting at the exact same table where, two weeks ago, Alex had started them on the path that had led him back here tonight. He hadn't intended to come here. In fact, he'd nearly been home when his courage deserted him, and he pulled off the road. Confusion, frustration, desolation crushed in on him until he felt as if he'd been buried alive.

He simply couldn't go home until he figured out a few of the tangled emotions choking him. He loved Alex and Allie. He was in love with them. As soon as the words had drifted through his mind in the truck, he'd tried to disregard the brunt force of that knowledge. Now as he sipped his beer, it ran over him like a two-ton freight train.

He loved both of them.

"Hey, stranger," a soft voice said, jarring him from his wayward thoughts.

"Brooks," he said, glancing up and finding Ginny smiling down at him. He looked over her shoulder, surprised to find her alone.

"Travers went back to our room. We spotted you when we walked in and he suggested I come sit with you. Silly man is plotting some surprise."

"So things between you and Travers are good?" he asked, leaning back. He and Brooks had been friends forever and a day and, despite the fact that he was nervous as hell about filling her in on his budding relationship with her sister, he was glad to see her. She was funny and fun, and he'd missed her the past couple weeks. She and Travers had been out of the office more than they'd been in it, but he figured they were entitled, considering they had let nearly twenty years of unrequited lust build up between them.

"Things with Travers are unbelievably good. Great, stupendous, astounding, breathtaking!"

Charlie chuckled at her enthusiasm. "I'm glad. You look really happy."

"I wish I could say the same for you. The little I've seen you this week, you've been walking around like Charlie Brown under his dark cloud. What gives?"

He shrugged, toying with the idea of confessing all. He felt like he needed some of Brooks' common sense wisdom. He'd been inundated with Alex and Allie's skewed view of the world nonstop for two weeks. He wanted to talk to someone with a solid grasp on reality.

"I'm having some relationship problems," he said, internally debating how many details to provide.

"You? Relationship problems? Get out!" Brooks replied, shoving his shoulder playfully.

"What's so unbelievable about that?" He felt a bit pissed off at her astonishment.

"Anderson, you've never let a woman get under your skin. Ever. I wondered if I'd ever see the day. So who's brought you to your knees? I want to go shake her hand."

Her smug teasing pushed him to retaliate. "Allie."

Brooks' smile dimmed a bit. "My sister Allie?"

Charlie nodded, finding his confession surprisingly easy. "I've been in love with her for years."

Brooks sat silent for so long, Charlie wondered if he'd struck her mute. Brooks was never quiet. "I always thought…"

"Thought what?" he asked.

"Nothing," she said, brushing her comment aside. "What does Taylor think of you and Allie?"

Now it was his turn to fall speechless. What could have prompted her question? Had Alex talked to Brooks about his feelings?

"Alex is okay with it," he answered vaguely.

"You're a terrible liar, Anderson. You always have been."

"What's that mean?"

"You called Taylor 'Alex'. Why don't you go ahead and tell me the whole sordid tale? If you and Allie have finally admitted your feelings, then why are you so blue? Why are you sitting here alone in a bar, drinking?"

"Alex is in love with her too," he added.

"I know."

"You know?" he asked, astonished to hear Brooks' admission.

"I saw him kiss her that night by the bonfire, years ago. Of course I also watched her drooling over you for nearly an hour prior to that. Next thing I know, she hits the open road with Griffin. I sort of suspected she was afraid of coming between the two of you, but Allie was uncharacteristically closed mouthed about her feelings."

Charlie nodded slowly, trying to let Brooks' words sink in. She thought her sister had run in order to avoid driving a wedge between him and Alex. He marveled over how Allie's departure six years ago could be misinterpreted by so many people, himself included.

After spending time with her, listening to her stories of her years away, he realized she'd made the right decision in leaving. She'd remained true to herself and, as a result, was able to return home the mature, wonderful woman he'd fallen in love with. He wondered how differently things might have turned out if she'd given in to Alex's proposal six years earlier. He couldn't shake the thought that he hadn't been ready for at least one part of Alex's desires back then. Over the course of the past six years, he and his friend had grown closer, and he suspected it was only their shared pasts, history, that had enabled him to take that step from friendship to lover.

It seems he'd grown up as well.

"So what's the end of the story, Anderson?"

The words flew from his mouth, slowly but steadily. He told Brooks everything that had happened since that first Friday here at the club, leaving out nothing. She listened in silence, nodding occasionally, but to her tribute, she never once looked shocked or horrified.

Only when he'd finished, explaining how he'd come to be sitting in this bar dealing with the realization that he was in love with both of them, did she speak.

"I don't understand why you're here," she said quietly, and he was jarred by her simple statement. He'd just confessed to entering into a ménage with her sister and a homosexual affair with their best friend.

"Jesus, Brooks, are you so out of your head in love that you haven't heard a word I just said?"

"Explain to me what you think the problem is."

Charlie shook his head. "And to think, you're the normal sister. You can't tell what might be bothering me?"

Brooks laughed at his question. "You've fallen in love and you've had the good fortune to have that love returned."

"Allie doesn't know about what happened in my office today. She doesn't know Alex and I have become lovers."

"You've known Allie since she was a little girl. Do you really think my anything-goes sister is going to have a problem with that? From what you've said, I get a feeling she's been guiding the two of you toward that event."

Charlie considered her words, recalling Allie's sudden loss of memory in the shower when she asked Alex to show her how to give him a hand job. And it was Allie who had encouraged him to kiss Alex on the couch. "You're right. She won't mind."

"So if that's not what's bothering you, what is?"

"How do I make a happily ever after with two people, Brooks? As you've just pointed out, I've never managed that feat with one person."

"You never settled down because you gave your heart to Taylor and Allie years ago. You just didn't realize it."

"It doesn't bother you that your sister is hooking up with two men? Two men who are also hooking up with each other?"

Brooks scowled at him. "Are you kidding me? If I could have picked any man on earth for Allie, it would have been you or Taylor. Lucky girl managed to land you both. I can honestly say my sister has the luck of the Irish."

"Crap, what's Allie done now?" Travers asked as he walked over and joined them at the table. "Won the lottery? Found another rich old man to fly her all over the world?"

"She's managed to get Anderson and Taylor to fall in love with her," Brooks replied, and Charlie fought the impulse to crawl under the table when Travers' head jerked toward him.

"And better yet," his former best friend continued, "Anderson and Taylor have finally admitted their feelings for each other. So all's well that ends well."

Travers sat silent for several moments and Charlie struggled to swallow past the nervous lump in his throat. It was one thing confessing his newfound relationship to Brooks. She was a woman, and females tended to be a bit more understanding about matters of the heart. Travers was a man's man, and he feared his friend would be more than a bit repulsed by the idea of him and Alex having sex…with each other.

Finally his friend nodded. "Are you happy, Anderson?" he asked.

Charlie leaned back and considered Travers' question. "Yeah," he said quickly. The question required no thought. Now that he contemplated it, he'd never been happier in his life. Talking to his friends had really put things in to perspective, and he wondered why he'd been so freaked out to begin with. Travers and Brooks' calm acceptance of his new relationship relieved some of his own fears. Love was all that mattered. He loved them and, God willing, they loved him back. He'd been a damn fool to hide from that fact.

Travers grinned at his response and Brooks giggled. "So I'll repeat my question, why are you here?" she asked.

"No reason," he answered with a smile. "No reason at all."

* * *

Charlie had settled his bar tab and was just about to head back to his truck when the doorman stopped him.

"Oh, Mr. Anderson. I have a message for you from Mr. Taylor."

Charlie took the note from the man and opened it.

It merely said, Your room. Here. Now. A & A

He grinned, pleased that he wouldn't have to make the long drive home. Now that he'd cast away his worries, he was ready to embark on the next step in this relationship. He'd been ready to grovel and beg for forgiveness. The fact that they were both here, waiting for him, gave him hope that they would forgive his foolish panic attack.

As he walked down the hallway to his private room, he fought down the excitement and anticipation. Tonight, he thought. Tonight it all comes together. Everything nice in the world was within his grasp.

Chapter Nine

The room was dark except for the single candle by the bed and the light flooding in from the hallway as Charlie entered the room rather tentatively. Alex watched his friend's entrance from the corner then glanced over quickly to make sure Allie was okay. Prior to sending the message to Charlie, he'd tied her spread-eagle to the bed at her request. Allie felt certain that perhaps they could put Charlie's unease to rest if they gave the man back some of the control over their unusual sexual desires.

Allie, to Alex's delight, confessed her fascination and curiosity regarding bondage. Thrilled by her willingness to experiment with one of his favorite sexual positions, Alex had happily complied with her request.

He'd decided to hang back for a little while, remaining in the dark shadows of the room until Charlie had seen Allie.

"What's going on?" Charlie asked when he spotted Allie on the bed. Seeing her naked had prompted his friend to quickly close the door lest someone in the hallway pass by and see her. By shutting the door, he'd also guaranteed that Alex could remain hidden.

"We love you," Allie said from the bed.

"'We'?" Charlie asked. For the first time Alex questioned the wisdom of their plan for virtual darkness. He couldn't discern from Charlie's voice how he felt about Allie's admission.

"Alex and I," she added softly. "We love you, Charlie."

His friend stepped closer to the bed, and at last Alex could see a bit of his face, though it was still cast in shadows.

"Where is Alex?" Charlie asked, and Alex's heart raced at the impatient tone of his friend's voice.

"Oh," Allie replied vaguely. "He's around."

"Hiding?" Charlie asked. "Too afraid to come out and face me?"

Alex felt Charlie's taunt in his gut, but hesitated in responding. He and Allie had intended for Charlie to take her up on her obvious invitation to play. The fact that he wasn't touching the woman he loved left Alex feeling unsure. Perhaps Charlie had decided their ménage was too much for him. Maybe he regretted their hot, hard lovemaking in the office. Again Alex cursed the darkness that kept Charlie's face from his view. If only he could see him, he thought.

"He's not afraid," Allie said with a sexy smile. "We thought perhaps you'd like to even the score, so to speak."

Her words obviously caught Charlie unaware as he glanced down at her. "Even the score?"

"You accused me of being a naughty girl in the truck a couple weeks ago, but I think you and Alex were the bad boys this afternoon," she teased. "I'm very angry with you for leaving me out. I told Alex it was only fair that I get to be with each of you…alone."

Charlie seemed to process her words. "And you and Alex?"

"We had sex together before arriving here. Damn man didn't like the outfit I originally planned to wear. Or maybe he liked it too much. Anyway, I don't think you can blame us, Charlie. You have been leaving us alone quite a lot lately."

"A habit I fully intend to break," Charlie muttered.

Allie giggled at his gruff words, and Alex reached down to grip his throbbing erection. He and Allie had completely undressed before Charlie's arrival. He slowly pulled his fist along his hard cock, fighting back a groan at the touch. He was overcome with the need to join them, fuck them, love them. God, so many emotions were working on his psyche, he didn't know which end was up. He only knew which body part was up. Way up. He tightened his grip and pulled his cock harder.

"Come to bed," Allie begged, and he watched as Charlie took in the image of their woman in bonds. The soft silk straps looked lovely against the pale skin around her ankles and wrists.

"Is this all for me?" Charlie asked, gesturing at her lovely body.

"Just you," Allie whispered.

Charlie unbuttoned his shirt, and Alex was certain neither he nor Allie were breathing, watching as their sexy man slowly drew out the process of undressing. In their brief time together, none of them had mastered the ability to leisurely enjoy the intimacies of foreplay. It appeared that tonight, Charlie meant to draw out the anticipation.

Damn him.

Allie shivered on the bed, and Alex struggled not to rush toward her, to touch her, to put her out of her agony. Fuck, to put himself out of his sexual distress. He'd never been harder or in more pain. Charlie's slow striptease was working on him like a whip against his back. Each blow building the pleasure with the pain.

"Charlie, please," Allie begged, but his friend didn't move. He looked down at Allie as if memorizing each precious curve of her body.

"I love you, Allie," Charlie said, his words unexpected yet as welcome as the sun after days of rain.

"Oh, Charlie," Allie whispered, and even from across the room Alex could see the sheen of happy tears in her eyes. "I love you too."

Charlie glanced around the dark room, and Alex was amazed when his friend's gaze seemed to find him even in the inky blackness.

"I love you, Alex. Now get your ass over here. I'm not in the mood for any more hiding."

Alex grinned and walked toward the bed. He looked across Allie's body at his best friend and suddenly felt like the richest man on earth.

"Okay?" he asked, still unable to truly believe he was standing in this room with the only two people he'd ever wanted in his life.

"Well, that depends. We seem to have a captive wildcat on our hands, and she's offering herself up for some kinky loving. Seems to me this might be a two-man job," Charlie answered with a sexy grin.

Glancing around, Alex studied Charlie's room. When they'd first arrived, he and Allie had marveled at the décor. Before tonight, he'd never seen Charlie's room at the Way Down Under Club. He knew Travers was fond of bondage and had heard his friend discuss some of the more interesting pieces of furniture in his room. He'd been amazed to discover that Charlie's room looked very much like his bedroom at home. Simple and chaste by sex-club standards. Aside from the collection of toys on the bedside table and the silk scarves attached to the bedposts, there'd been nothing else in the room besides a desk and comfortable chaise lounge.

Charlie chuckled and he knew his friend was aware of his confusion. "Sex is all in the mind," Charlie said. "Everything else is superfluous." As he spoke, Charlie reached down and untied Allie's legs.

"Hey," she protested, a question in the single word.

"Not tonight, Allie-cat," Charlie murmured, leaning down to kiss her lips. "No games. No pretending. Just the three of us with all the masks off, all the walls down."

Alex released her hands, watching as Charlie deepened the kiss and crawled onto the bed, over her body. Unable to watch and remain apart from them, Alex reached down and ran his hand over Charlie's muscular back. He was thrilled to feel his friend's shiver of delight.

"Help me," he heard Allie plead, and he knew her desire was reaching fever pitch. The bondage, though brief, had been working its way through her body in a glorious way, and Alex couldn't wait to experiment more with that knowledge another night.

"Patience," he heard Charlie murmur against her mouth despite the fact he was spreading her legs and positioning his cock at her hot, wet entrance. Alex realized they were all fighting a losing battle. Not once had they managed to deny themselves what they'd all waited years to experience. The time for finesse and foreplay would come once the haste, the newness, wore off.

Maybe, Alex thought with a grin. Hopefully.

As Charlie slowly pushed into Allie, Alex moved into position behind his friend. He wondered if Charlie would balk at his choice, at his intimate location, and silently cheered when Charlie thrust his ass back toward him. The idea that his best friend would give himself to him this way, so freely, so easily, moved Alex beyond words. The trust and commitment between them had grown to such proportions Alex felt his heart would burst with bliss.

"Hurry," Allie said to him, her gaze on his as he knelt, spellbound, behind Charlie. "All of us together. Please, Alex."

Alex hastily grabbed the new tube of lubrication he'd found earlier. Donning a condom and coating it with the gel, he pushed the tube gently into his friend's ass, squirting a generous amount.

"Christ," Charlie muttered when Alex slid a finger into the tight portal. "I can't believe I'm letting you do this to me."

Allie giggled until Charlie thrust inside her once again, harder. "Oh my God," she sighed.

"Allie-cat. I'm warning you right now. If you come without permission, I'm taking you over my knee and spanking your impatient ass," Charlie threatened.

"And when he's finished, hellion, I'm taking a turn. I'm in no hurry to see this end."

Charlie hissed when Alex added yet another finger, pounding inside his friend's ass several times, stretching the tight muscles.

When he felt he had to get inside his friend or die, Alex removed his fingers and positioned himself at the entrance. He paused for a moment, waiting for Charlie to resist or change his mind. His resistance was shattered when Charlie pushed back slowly on his hard cock until just the thick crest of the head made its way in.

"Shit," he murmured, terrified of screwing up, of turning Charlie off.

"Alex," his friend murmured, obviously aware of his distress. "Little more, if you don't mind."

Alex laughed at his words and pushed forward slowly, bit by bit, until he was lodged balls-deep inside Charlie's ass. All three of them stopped, seemingly astounded by the powerful emotions evoked by the moment.

Allie recovered first. "Move," she whimpered. "And Charlie—hard and fast, if you please."

Alex smiled at her words. He'd revealed his suspicions regarding Charlie's somewhat reserved lovemaking. He felt his friend jerk at her request, but other than that he remained motionless.

"Hard and fast," she repeated. "Both of you."

Her words were the impetus, and Alex was overwhelmed by Charlie's powerful thrusts. He slid out slightly as Charlie pounded into Allie, struggling to hold off his orgasm, and Charlie slammed back against his rock-hard flesh on his retreat from their lady-love's body. Over and over they moved together, the three of them, in perfect unison. A perfect trio.

Charlie was the first to surrender to his desire, his hard climax triggering Alex's and Allie's.

As they lay together in the aftermath, Alex knew that they'd made it through the dangers, the traps, the tricks. The stage was set, the plot written, the roles ready to be cast—and he couldn't wait to see who ended up with what part.

ABOUT THE AUTHOR

Writing a book was number one on Mari Carr's bucket list. Now her computer is jammed full of stories — novels, novellas, short stories and dead-ends. A *New York Times* and *USA TODAY* bestseller, Mari finds time for writing by squeezing it into the hours between 3 a.m. and daybreak when her family is asleep.

You can visit Mari's website at www.maricarr.com. She is also on Facebook and Twitter.

Look for these titles by Mari Carr

Big Easy:

Blank Canvas

Crash Point

Full Position

Rough Draft

Triple Beat

Winner Takes All

Going Too Fast

Boys of Fall:

Free Agent

Red Zone

Wild Card

Compass:

Northern Exposure

Southern Comfort

Eastern Ambitions

Western Ties

Winter's Thaw

Hope Springs

Summer Fling

Falling Softly

Foreign Affairs:

Princess

Cowboy

Master

Hands

June Girls:

No Recourse

No Regrets

Just Because:

Because of You

Because You Love Me

Because It's True

Lowell High:

Bound by the Past

Covert Affairs

Mad about Meg

Bundles

Cowboy Heat

Sugar and Spice

Madison Girls

Scoundrels

Second Chances:

Fix You

Full Moon

Status Update

The Back-Up Plan

Never Been Kissed

Say Something

Sparks in Texas:

Sparks Fly

Waiting for You

Something Sparked

Off Limits

No Other Way

Whiskey Eyes

Trinity Masters:

Elemental Pleasure

Primal Passion

Scorching Desire

Forbidden Legacy

Hidden Devotion

Elegant Seduction

Secret Scandal

Wild Irish:

Come Monday

Ruby Tuesday

Waiting for Wednesday

Sweet Thursday

Friday I'm in Love

Saturday Night Special

Any Given Sunday

Wild Irish Christmas

January Girl

Individual Titles:

Seducing the Boss

Tequila Truth

Erotic Research

Rough Cut

Happy Hour

Power Play

One Daring Night

Assume the Positions

Slam Dunk

Manufactured by Amazon.ca
Bolton, ON

35729130R00166